'13

The Sum of

Our Gods

BENJAMIN GORMAN

NOT
a
PIPE
Publishing

Copyright © 2013 by Benjamin Gorman

The text of this book is in Garamond. The title and copyright are in Diogenes by Apostrophic Labs. Chapter numbers are in ROMAN SD by Steve Deffeyes.

Author's Note: All characters in this book should be considered fictional with the exceptions of Andy and Denise, who have given their permission to have their real names used. As for the various gods, they should be considered fictional or real depending on which you (and they) find least offensive.

For Paige and Noah,
My Reasons

1

In the beginning, there was a bell.

It hung on a hook above the door, and when Yahweh pushed His way into Andy's Cafe it rang, causing Joe to look up from the counter at God, creator of the Universe, the Great I Am, schlepping His way around the empty tables in the small dining area.

"How's it going?" Joe asked. Though dressed in his usual middle-management suit, Joe Miller looked like someone who could model camping gear. His jawline said, "C'mon, guys, we can tough this out," and the crow's feet that appeared near his eyes when he smiled said, "Who's up for some s'mores?" He hadn't been camping for years, though, and lately his smiles were rare and a bit sadder than burnt-marshmallows.

God grunted as He sat heavily on the stool next to Joe. The waitress, Andy's wife, Denise, brought out Yahweh's usual. Coffee. Black. And some silverware wrapped in a paper napkin that he never touched. Yahweh acknowledged Denise with a nod, but He didn't smile, either. His current disguise consisted of old-man clothes and a Santa Clause beard flowing out of his longish white hair. But his eyes didn't foreshadow any bowl-full-of-jelly belly laughs. Instead, they advertised that, at any minute, he might shout, "You shall not pass!" and smash a bridge or something.

When Denise went back into the kitchen, Yahweh heard the tinny sound coming from the little radio sitting on a shelf near the stove. Joan Osborne sang, "What if God was one of us…"

Joe followed Yahweh's gaze into the kitchen, then heard the music. He bit down on a smile and shot Yahweh a glance.

Yahweh sneered. "I fucking hate this song."

He pushed out the word "fucking" with such passion that, at a point in the Indian Ocean just south of South Africa, on the exact opposite side of the Earth, sea beds shifted enough to cause a tsunami that would do millions of dollars' worth of damage to the cities of Port Elizabeth, Boknes, and Kenton-on-the-Sea, but with no reported fatalities. Significantly farther to the south, an as-of-yet undiscovered but inhabited planet shifted in its rotation around another medium-sized star, raising its surface temperature by 357.4 degrees and wiping out all its plants and animals. But what are you going to do? It's a terrible song. And God hated it the most.

"So," Joe asked God, "have you made a decision about that thing we talked about?"

"You mean the thing you bring up every week?"

Joe sipped his coffee. "Yeah. That."

"No."

"No?"

"No, I haven't made up my mind. I'll let you know when I decide. So you can quit asking."

But Yahweh knew Joe would keep reminding him. It was, after all, Joe's single greatest concern in life, and understandably so. Secretly, Yahweh was glad Joe kept mentioning it, because He was getting a lot more forgetful than He liked to admit.

"In that case, how's the family?" Joe asked.

"Ugh. Where to start? Have you noticed how everything is changing so fast? I mean, there's always some shifting going on. Some drama. But it used to take centuries, millennia even, for somebody to make a big move. Now it seems like somebody's up and somebody's down, and the next day it shifts. I can hardly keep the family politics straight."

"You know, I used to think that feeling that things are going faster was just a function of old age," Joe said. "But now it feels real to me. It does seem like things are speeding up, objectively speaking. But then, I am getting older. I have no basis of comparison. Am I just getting old?"

Yahweh snorted. "You're what? 35? Gimme a break. Talk to me in a few thousand years."

Joe sat up quickly. "Seriously? You won't leave me alone once I'm dead?"

Yahweh shook his head slightly as he reached for his coffee cup. "I was kidding. I won't bug you in Hel."

"I'm going to Hell?" Joe asked. He didn't sound too surprised or scared, considering.

"Hel. One 'L.' The Underworld. It's not all gnashing of teeth and sulfur and Dante's Inferno decor. Really peaceful, actually. Like a vacation where you rent a cabin, and then it rains, so you don't have anything you need to go out and do."

"Doesn't sound too bad."

"It's no Asgard, but then, you don't have all the politics. 'Course, you might not go to Hel. Maybe Freyja will pick you to go to Folkvangr."

"What's that like?" Joe asked.

Yahweh frowned. "Don't know. Never bothered to check it out. I don't really care much about the dead. They're boring as all get-out."

"Lacking a certain joie de vivre?" Joe asked, totally dry.

Yahweh smiled. "No get-up-and-go, those people."

"But there is an afterlife?" Joe asked more seriously.

Yahweh pretended to tap a cigar like Groucho Marx. "If you call that livin'!"

Joe knew when he was being told to give up on the line of questioning. They'd been down that road before.

After a pause, Joe asked, "So, how's the wife?"

"Frigga? Still hardly ever talks to me. I know I'm supposed to joke that this is some kind of mitzvah, but I like it about as much as I like...." Yahweh trailed off.

"What?"

"I was going to make a kosher joke. Raw shellfish. Bacon-wrapped sushi. Menstruating sheep. But I know you won't get it."

"I'm not Jewish," Joe said. "How many times do I have to tell you?"

"Your mother is Jewish. Dayenu. That would be enough. But your father was mine, too. One pretty lapsed Hebrew, that guy, but still mine. And her mother was Jewish, and his mother was Jewish. I'm like your student loan officer; you can't run away from me, buddy."

"My dad raised me to be an atheist," Joe reminded Yahweh.

"Yet he knew you'd be sitting here one day. Was that his sense of humor, or was he a real dick?"

"One and the same, my friend. One and the same." Joe took a sip of his coffee. "It's your fault, too. You made him bitter." Joe pointed at Yahweh's coffee. "You like bitter."

Yahweh shrugged. "Sometimes. I waffle."

"You're the dick," Joe muttered under his breath.

"Joseph, watch yourself," Yahweh warned. "You're reverting. Your dad liked to talk to me about you, you know. I know all about the teenage Joe."

"You know my dad's perspective."

"Between his and Mine, that's pretty good."

Joe looked at Yahweh. "Touché."

They drank their coffees in silence for a moment.

Joe caved first. "So Frigga hardly talks to you. What about the boy?"

"Jesus? He doesn't talk to anybody. Hasn't done much but grunt in almost two millennia. Just sits on that old, stinky corduroy couch of his. I wish I never gave that to him. It was a gift, you know, to try and make him feel better. That was back when his whole project went south."

"When was that?"

"337. Found out his wife was bangin' another guy. He just fell apart. I thought the couch would be a good gesture. You know, it doesn't say, 'It's no big deal. Get over it,' like a new red convertible. I wanted to be sensitive, in a kind of Bill Clinton 'I feel your pain' kind'a way."

"Well, what can you do?"

"Yeah. But it's been 1,673 years. And Inanna, my daughter-in-law, she's been whoring it up with everybody and his brother ever since. Maybe it's time for that red convertible now, uh?"

"Think so?" Joe asked.

"I don't know. I wanted to be close to Jesus, but the kid's never made all that much sense to me. All that love and no smiting. We just don't have that much in common. You ever feel that way with your son?"

"No, not really," Joe said. "Dawkins and I are really close. I mean, he's only seven, so it's still pretty easy for a dad. I expect it will get harder during the teenage years."

"It does," Yahweh interrupted. "It really does. Long before Jesus, I had other kids, you know. Not just the other gods, but ones that were really Mine."

"You mean, like, biologically?"

"Well, it doesn't really work that way. But they were higher than the other gods. 'Sat on the right hand of God the Father' and all that."

"And what happened?"

"Tried to kill Me. Every one of the little bastards. Had to smite 'em all. Lotsa smiting back then. Some casting down, too. You know, tossing them in the pit of Tartarus or demoting them to normal god slash demon status. Even had to eat some of them. Not pleasant. Certainly not kosher."

"I bet."

"Yeah. Dawkins will probably want to pop you in the jaw someday, but he'll never try to kill you. So there's that."

"Yeah, there's that," Joe said.

Yahweh sipped his coffee. "Andy?" He called into the kitchen.

Andy pushed the swinging door out with his foot and poked his head through. "Yeah?"

"Your coffee is terrible."

Andy smiled. "You love it."

"My favorite in the whole world."

Andy nodded and disappeared into the kitchen.

Yahweh turned to Joe. "I think it's getting worse."

"You say that every week."

"I know. It's getting worse every week."

"And that's why you like it," Joe said. He'd obviously been through this before.

Yahweh took another sip. "Mmm. So bitter."

They sat in silence again.

"So is Inanna still plotting with…what was his name?" Joe asked.

"Which one?"

"Um, god of air and political discourse, I think."

Yahweh nodded, then shook his head. "Enlil. Yeah, um, no, I don't think so. Not as much anymore, though you never can tell with her. But she seems to be working more with Daikokuten."

"What's he god of?"

"Wealth."

"Makes sense."

"S'not like our positions are that fixed, though. Before she was goddess of the Church, Inanna used to just be some minor fertility goddess. Like you said, Enlil was a god of air."

"But you've always been in charge?"

"Oh, hell no. I worked my way up, and I've been up and down. Lotsa maneuvering. That's what it's all about."

"But you are The Creator, right? You made the universe."

"Pretty much. But so what? The guy who put up the drywall in your house, does he tell you what to do? In Egypt I was Amun, and I wasn't in charge. Ra was my boss. But the Hebrews, they were builders, so I worked with them. You know, a god of creation with a bunch of laborers. Makes sense, right? Most folks preferred Ra, the god of the sun. Horus worked with the Pharaohs, so he was making a move on Ra. But I took my people and high-tailed it. Spent a long time duking it out with Hadad, the Baalite god of fertility and agriculture. Inanna's uncle. Eventually came out on top."

"Are you still on top?"

Yahweh took another sip of his coffee. "I'm honestly not sure. Maybe? Maybe Inanna and whoever she's working with will have me demoted and sharing a room in the old gods' assisted living community with Hadad by next week."

Joe frowned. "How bad could that be?"

Yahweh shrugged. "Hadad isn't such a bad guy. Kind of simple, but he knows how to party."

"I mean for us."

Yahweh turned and looked at Joe, genuinely surprised. "I hadn't thought about that. I really don't know." He gently elbowed Joe, then made a dismissive gesture with His free hand while taking another sip of His coffee. "'Worry not for tomorrow, for'…it will most likely be pretty much the same as today. A tiny bit different. Maybe a little better. Who knows?" Then God frowned.

"What?" Joe asked.

"I know who knows. Frigga knows. I think I'll try to get that out of her." Yahweh took one last sip of his coffee, set the cup down gently on the bar, and started to stand.

"Hey, um, do you think you could also ask her when you're going to have an answer for me about that thing we talked about."

God winked at Joe. "Maybe, Joe. Have a good week. I'll see ya next week."

Joe leaned to one side and pulled his wallet out of his back pocket. "Okay. I'll see ya."

While Joe paid, God shuffled over to the door without looking back. He took a few steps out, and, when he thought no one was looking, He ascended into heaven.

2

There may actually have been a time when small towns
afforded people a tighter community than any that could be
found in a big city, but the conjoined cities of Independence
and Monmouth, Oregon, with a combined population of
16,000, had enough privacy fences and Facebook accounts to
keep the residents as isolated from their neighbors as anyone
living in a suburb of America's great metropolises. Sure, it was
a lot easier to strike up a conversation with the mayor on a
street corner in Independence, but people's spheres were small
and self-selected: nuclear families, coworkers, political
partisans, connections made at kids' soccer games, at one of
the 17 churches, at school board meetings or the Rotary club.

The Future Farmers of America Annual Banquet and Auction may have been a bigger deal in Independence/Monmouth than it would have been in San Francisco or Boston, but when people locked their doors and played Angry Birds on their iPads, they were just as alone as everyone else. Consequently, a stranger stepping out of a greasy spoon on Main Street didn't turn any heads, and as long as people couldn't see Him ascend into Heaven, they didn't care that He might be disappearing from their lives forever. A stranger is a stranger, after all.

The stranger didn't notice the townspeople, either. Casual disinterest isn't very alarming, and people in disguise don't take particular note of those fooled by their masks. Plus, God didn't have a very attuned sense for those instances when He was being watched. Some people are always looking for God, but He'd lost interest in being found. It had been a long time since His days of appearing as pillar of cloud and His nights of appearing as a pillar of fire. With all those eyes searching in vain, it's easy to understand why he didn't notice another pair watching Him as He slipped out of Andy's Cafe.

Across the street, leaning against a nondescript sedan (Was that a Hyundai Sonata? A Nissan Versa? A Chevy Cruze?) stood a late twenty-something hipster smoking a cigarette. His t-shirt said, "I Am Not Here." The assassin, disguised as the hipster, watched Yahweh, disguised in his "Manny" costume, take a few steps out onto the sidewalk, then disappear.

The assassin pointed a pair of finger guns at the spot where God had vanished. "Pew-pew," he said. He blew imaginary smoke from the barrels and holstered his hands in his pockets. "He didn't even look around to make sure no one saw him," Meme muttered. "The old God is getting sloppy."

The assassin dropped the half-smoked cigarette into the gutter, stepped on it and twisted his foot, then turned and climbed into the rental. After scanning the street to make sure it was completely deserted at that early morning hour, he sloughed off his hipster disguise completely. The lips that had held the cigarette evaporated, as did the eyes that he'd used to spy on God.

Meme was the god of postmodern evangelical atheism. While other gods put on flesh and vestments that spoke to their particular purviews, Meme had no face or distinguishing physical characteristics at all. Smooth as a baby's bottom, some might say. His skin was a foggy gray that created an optical illusion, looking, at any angle, like something that had been digitally concealed. This floating, out-of-focus mannequin, basically Gort, the giant Cyclops robot from The Day the Earth Stood Still only smaller and with one less eye, looked like a being that didn't want to be distinguishable in any way.

Meme had previously been a minor deity, his atheism giving him dominion over only a few intellectuals scattered across the globe. In the age of post-modernism, when the sign had been officially divorced from the signified and everything turned in on itself as an ironic reference, Meme had inspired a new kind of evangelical atheist who would go out into the world preaching the certainty of the non-existence of God (any god) with just as much religious fervor as the most zealous fundamentalist. And the more these evangelists converted, the stronger Meme became. But the more religious they became about their atheism, the more ironic Meme grew. His hipster in an "I Am Not Here" t-shirt became a disguise based on a memory, but his new, true form was this piece of modern-art physical deflection.

For such a seemingly complex god, Meme's singular goal was simple: he wanted to put an end to the gods. It got tricky because he was one of the gods himself. He had to undo God's dominion without doing anything divine, lest he replace Yahweh as the new Lord of the Universe. For now, he could only watch and sneer. Looking down his nose at things was Meme's equivalent of hope, fittingly ironic since he had no nose.

This do-nothing strategy seemed to be working. Yahweh's attentions were focused on this ridiculous curse. Meme looked (as much as a being with no eyes can look) through the window of Andy's at the human still sitting at the counter. Meme didn't care about the reason Joe was cursed as long as the weekly meetings kept Yahweh busy. He understood the curse. Meme knew the event that had earned God's wrath. He understood that betrayal served as an outsized sin in Yahweh's antiquated, tribal moral schema. Meme found the curse to be a ridiculous waste of time, but that didn't make him feel any sympathy for the human. Meme just didn't care. He also knew about the betrayal that Inanna planned to execute, and it made the cause of Joe's curse look paltry by comparison.

Meme had been watching Inanna, too, and he knew her plot was moving forward. Meme could let her try to undermine God, try to take His place, and in the process there was a good chance they would both lose enough power to control the lives of the humans. Meme had watched Inanna's pet project, that Not-Normal man in Paris, and thought the plan just might work, but he hoped (sneered) that it would also backfire on the Baalite fertility goddess herself. Meme hoped it would turn people away from anything divine. Sure, the gods didn't depend on human worship for survival. Prayers weren't god-food. But if creation itself could reject its Creator, maybe that would put an end to a relationship Meme saw as antiquated, patriarchal, and imperialistic. Maybe God would just wither under the weight of His own pointlessness. Maybe He'd retire to the old gods' assisted living community with Zeus, Ra, Shiva, Odin, and the other gods who'd given up on the corporate rat race. Or maybe He'd just die.

Meme considered squealing to express his excitement, but decided against it. He was a god of few words. (He had lot of thoughts built out of a pretentious, inflated vocabulary but, unlike his acolytes, he graciously kept most of them to himself.) Still, he couldn't resist the urge to drum his thumbs on the wheel of the car, a rhythmic thrumming to match his eagerness. To Meme, the choice to attempt the assassination of Yahweh didn't have moral weight. No choice was "right" or "wrong." For that matter, sitting on the sidelines while Innana helped her Not-Normal man wasn't an act of criminal negligence, either. That didn't faze him a bit. But the idea of killing god gave Meme a boner.

He put the key in the ignition and started the car. He knew he had to beat Yahweh back to the board meeting or he'd arouse suspicion, and God's obsession with this one solitary human was Meme's biggest advantage. He dropped the car into drive and accelerated to Heaven. He punched the presets on the little car's radio and hummed along to John Lennon's "Imagine."

It might not be right or wrong, but trying to off the supreme deity of the universe was going to be pretty fun.

3

While Joe climbed into his '95 Nissan Maxima for his short commute to the Prudential Investment store at the strip mall, Yahweh made His own commute back to the office where He worked. Like many offices, Asgard looked better from a distance than it did up close.

As Yahweh passed through various dimensions (moving, at one point, up, so that the term "ascend" is technically correct), Asgard came into focus. From a distance it looked like a giant mountain floating in a black void, with a bright light shining on the top. Even after all these millennia, Yahweh was still pleased with how it had come out. Most of the mountain wore a coat of bright green grasses and flowering bushes. Wispy clouds circled around it like half-halos. At its base, dark stones spread out like petticoats hanging in the nothingness, flowing up and down slightly. Near the top, that same dark color reappeared, dotted with snow. Perched on the peak, the City sent bright light out into the void.

As Yahweh moved closer, the details of the City revealed themselves, and He felt the usual disappointment. Suburbs of great gray buildings, their wide windows reflecting so much light, seemed like such a good idea at the time, but now they looked to Him like terrestrial government housing projects. Between them, the streets of gold glowed. Yahweh had long ago come to terms with the fact that gold streets were a design flaw. For one thing, the soft metal scratched too easily. Also, as there was no independent light source in this dimension, He'd had to shine light on them. When that proved impractical, He'd lit them from the bottom, using gold leaf to cover the light source, so that gold light shot out of the streets themselves. This seemed liked an elegant solution, and looked very pretty, but it blinded most travelers on the roads, and they really needed all their faculties because the smooth gold also caused them to slip all the time. Ultimately, the various gods, seraphim, demons, and other denizens of Asgard chose to fly around The City instead of using the roads. The dead, who couldn't fly, even in their new bodies, basically had to stay home or risk breaking a hip every time they went out.

Oh well, Yahweh thought for the millionth time, the best laid plans of mice and gods, I suppose. Nobody's perfect.

Like the other gods, Yahweh floated above His ill-conceived streets of gold, between the blocky buildings at the edges of Asgard. As His reflection flashed in one of the large apartment windows, He realized something.

18

"Crap," He muttered. "Almost forgot."

Yahweh was still wearing the face and body of "Manny," the intentionally innocuous old man who visited Andy's Café for a cup of coffee with the human, Joe Miller. For these visits, He'd chosen a head of thick gray hair, sideburns just a bit longer than was fashionable, somewhat wild white eyebrows, and a face so deeply lined that it couldn't ever be completely clean shaven. The body was stocky, a bit on the paunchy side, with comically skinny legs. At His full height, "Manny" stood at 5'10", but He was always hunched over a bit.

But gods changed faces and bodies as a means of communication. Humans had learned to change clothes, make-up, and even body dysmorphic jewelry long ago from their gods, though, in this respect at least, humans were at their most divine when they attended costume parties and tried to reveal themselves through elaborate masks and costumes. Yahweh always liked a good costume party. They were like Valhalla, like work, but without the pressure to do anything.

Today Yahweh wanted to convey authority, wisdom, and a kind of dangerous reserve, like He could snap at any minute. He chose a much younger face, very angular, with a square jaw and sharp cheekbones. He put on a neatly trimmed, close-cut black goatee and short black hair, straight but slightly combed back. He decided on a light-olive skin tone, something Azerbaijani or Chechen. For eyes, He chose to shape them like a woman's from southern Spain, but He painted the irises a bright Irish green. He went with a Mexican woman's long eyelashes, and painted His eyelids a soft blue.

Yahweh considered an alien body, perhaps some extra arms, or tree roots instead of legs, but decided on a humanoid form. He stretched it out to a triangular, cartoonish degree, with unnaturally wide and angular shoulders pointing down to small feet. Dressed in a black button-up shirt and slacks, he looked like an exclamation point with a head. All together, the body said, "Don't fuck with me today." God hoped it would work.

In the center of the City, He floated over the White Gate. It wasn't "Pearly." He'd always hated that name. It sounded oddly matronly, like something invented by a small-town spinster librarian. The White Gate was a symbolic piece of modern art, a white marble arch standing in the central square of the city. There were no doors on the gate, and no fence on either side. He wasn't a big fan of the piece. As modern art went, the symbolism was pretty pedestrian.

Yahweh watched the newly dead mulling around the square below, passing under the White Gate, examining it like tourists, their feet slipping on the smooth gold underneath. Pedestrian. Yahweh chuckled at His little pun.

Yahweh landed on the other side of the street. Well, almost. The little feet were hardly weight bearing, and taking individual steps on them would destroy the whole aesthetic of the body He'd chosen. Instead, He floated down to a comfortable hovering altitude of three inches when He was in front of the giant office building. A neo-gothic horizontal arch of riveted beams hung out over the doorway like a pursed upper lip. Standing on top, in matching metal letters, in a very corporate sans-serif font, it said, "VALHALLA."

Two of His assistants were waiting at the doors, which they opened in unison.

"Uriel." Yahweh nodded to the one who looked like a bodyguard.

"Sir," the burly seraph said. His 16 wings were wrapped tightly over his thick frame, so they could almost be mistaken for a leathery toga. While he held the door with one massive, muscled arm, with his clawed fingers wrapped around the oversized handle, he kept his other arm hidden under his wings, probably concealing some terrible weapon.

Yahweh turned to the other. "Gabriel. What's on deck for today?"

Gabriel had grown feathers on his wings, and he let them hang open and beautiful around a boring gray suit. He wore a white shirt and a thin black tie, but when Yahweh frowned at these, the shirt turned black, and his tie became bright purple.

"Better?" Gabriel asked.

Yahweh nodded and they stepped into the foyer. Well, the angels walked. Uriel's claws made high-pitched clicks on the marble floor, and Gabriel's shiny shoes made a much lower clap. Yahweh floated silently.

Gabriel looked at his clipboard and spoke to Yahweh's back. "Inanna has that presentation to make at nine. Then you have a board meeting at ten. Nothing too major. Some quarterly reports of some of the smaller branches to go over. Then lunch with Frigga, her friend Isis, and Isis' husband Osiris."

Yahweh groaned. "That guy is so boring."

"Yessir," Gabriel said. "Frigga said it would be a long lunch. At two you have a meeting with Mnevis, a founding partner of the firm Menthu, Naunet, and Mnevis. Some legal thing. Afternoon meeting with Jesus. Dinner with Frigga at home."

"No evening events?"

"Nothing on the calendar yet, sir."

"Well, that's a relief. This presentation of Inanna's. What's it about?"

"She didn't say, specifically. She said you'd find it… um…" He read from his notes: "…'amusing,' sir."

21

"'Amusing'? Hmm. What do you think, Gabriel? Do you think she's making her move?"

"I'm sure she's making a move. But not on her own."

"Right. Look, can you make some calls, find out who she's been fraternizing with most recently?"

"Certainly, sir."

Yahweh nodded to the seraphim sitting behind the information desk as they passed, but He didn't speak to them. There was no one else in the cavernous lobby, but Yahweh knew the floors above would be teeming with angels, gods, demons, and other assorted immortals.

At the far side of the large room, Uriel pulled one arm out of his cloak of wings and pushed the button for one of the elevators with a sharp, black claw. The doors slid open immediately. It always made Yahweh just a little bit happier when He didn't have to wait for an elevator. He was an impatient God.

As they positioned themselves in the elevator and the doors slid closed, His brief joy faded. He thought about Inanna's "amusing" presentation. He had a feeling it was going to be a terrible Goddamned day.

4

Time doesn't behave consistently across dimensions, or even within them. That's mostly because Chronos, the god of time, is easily distracted, more than a bit incompetent, and afflicted with irritable bowel syndrome. Also, some complex physics is involved. Consequently, while Yahweh rode the elevator up toward his office, Joe parked his Nissan Maxima in his driveway, stepped out, and walked up the concrete path toward his front door. He'd just finished an eight-hour-day.

The house itself was only a bit older than Dawkins. Joe and Christy had purchased it, brand new, when they found out Christy was pregnant and decided their rented row house within earshot of the train tracks would be less than ideal for a baby. They'd met the builders and were on a first-name basis. Joe and Christy secretly believed they'd been given a sweetheart deal on the house because the builders had been won over by Joe and Christy's winning personalities. Once they'd moved in, knowing the builders' first names allowed Christy to curse Jerry and Bob every time another little defect appeared. Mostly she called them "Dumbass and Dumber-ass" when she told people to run for the hills rather than buying from them.

The house hit all the suburban high notes: a picture window looking out over the small front lawn, marble for all the countertops, hardwood on the main floor, three bedrooms with a large bath off the master complete with a double sink and a spa tub. But the cheap panes in the picture window had leaked, losing their gas and replacing it with a misty fog. The marble countertops may or may not have been marble after all, but they were coated with some veneer that became permanently discolored by the rings from cold glasses. At one point, one of the double sinks in the master bath stopped working (Christy's side) and Joe had to cut a hole in the wall behind the cupboards underneath to discover Jerry and Bob's creative ideas about plumbing. The big spa tub might have been cool, except that if you ran the jets it leaked. They gave up on the jets after the second time they replaced part of the ceiling in the garage.

Despite these constant reminders about the danger of a deal that's too good to be true, Christy and Joe had come to love the house. In a way, every repair made it more their own, and because of Jerry and Bob's incompetence, every stud, piece of drywall, and pipe would be theirs before they paid off the 30-year mortgage. Besides the constant repairs, Christy expressed her pride in the house by carefully choosing which books would show on the shelves she hung in aesthetically pleasing places around the first floor. She camouflaged the books she was less proud of in her office at the college, where the sheer volume could hide an embarrassing spine. Joe decorated the house with small prints of his favorite paintings. He'd paint the walls behind the paintings in some more muted color that matched the painting, then mat the painting in a wide white border to match Christy's bookshelves. The effect was handsome, and it served as an eloquent expression of Joe's artistic self-concept; he was not an artist but a reverent art fan.

The wall just inside the door was painted a soft, sage yellow to match the large bush in the background of Claude Monet's "Corner of the Garden at Montgeron." Joe, unaware of his strict after-work routine, did exactly what he always did as he stepped into the house. He set his briefcase down just inside the door, near the bench that held an assortment of pairs of shoes. He hung his Western Oregon University jacket from the hook above said shoes. He loosened his tie and unbuttoned the top button of his shirt. He forgot to take his shoes off. And he called for his son.

From the kitchen, Christy could identify every element of the routine by the sound. The deadbolt made a click, followed by the inverted squish of the weather stripping around the door. Then the door closed, and the briefcase made its two sonorous bumps on the hardwood. She didn't like that he set it there but didn't fight it. She could even hear the soft sound of the jacket zipper tapping on the wall as he hung it up, and she imagined the sound of his tie and top button.

"Dawkins?" Joe called down the hall. He'd painted the walls of the hallway a cool gray-blue that matched the walls in

Cezanne's "Rideau, Cruchon et Compotier," which showed some brightly colored fruit including lemons and yellow peaches that complemented Monet's gardenscape.

"Shoes," Christy called back, just softly enough to not be confrontational.

Thump. Slide. Thump. Slide.

Before Christy could step into the hall, their son raced past, moving too fast for socked feet on hardwood floors.

She imagined she could hear him sliding into his father's side. The imaginary sound was just like his tie and top button.

As Christy turned into the gray hall, she saw Joe pick up Dawkins.

"Heavy D! How was your day?"

Dawkins was thin and gangly, like his dad at age seven. The nickname came from some rapper from the late eighties and early nineties who never made his way into either of their CD collections, but who made it into their memories nonetheless. When Dawkins got too big to carry comfortably, Joe called him the name once, Christy laughed, and that was that.

"Good," Dawkins said. "At recess, in four square, I was server the whole time. No one could beat me. I didn't do so good after lunch, though."

"Still!" Joe said. "All of morning recess. That's like, what, 15 minutes straight? How many people do you think you knocked back into the line?"

Dawkins shrugged. "Like 30."

"That's quite a run. Nice job." Joe carried Dawkins down the hall and dropped the boy onto his back on the couch. Then Joe sat down next to him. "Now what about school-school? What did you learn today?"

Christy smiled. She knew what was coming and liked this part of the routine.

"Nothing."

"What?" Joe shouted, smiling but drawing his face into a ridiculous, exaggerated mask.

Dawkins laughed. "Just kidding, Dad."

"Oh, phew! Okay, so what did you learn?"

"Did you know the National Anthem is about the war of 1812?"

"I did know that. Did you learn the words?"

"Not all of them."

"Okay, well, here's what I want you to find out for me tomorrow. How many sentences is the national anthem?"

"I don't know."

"Me neither. Find that out for me tomorrow, okay?"

"Okay, Dad." With that, Dawkins turned back toward the TV and settled himself into a nest of Spongebob and the pushy marketing of sugared cereal and plastic action figures.

Joe walked into the kitchen. One of its walls wore the soft blue of Monet's "Impression, Sunrise," which hung above the sink. The small area above the oven, underneath the cabinetry, was painted the bright orange of the sun from the same painting. Joe wasn't sure he liked it, especially the orange, and thought about hanging Picasso's "Bread and Fruit Dish on a Table" and repainting the walls, one dark green and one the white of the draped napkin and bowls. It would be a more appetizing painting, anyway. "How about you, hon'?" he asked Christy. "What did you learn at school today?"

Christy smiled. "Nuh-thin'," she drawled. She was a pretty woman by anyone's standards, but especially beautiful to Joe, even though he hadn't noticed that she'd lost five pounds on her current diet and had her shoulder-length brown hair brown hair layered so that it stayed straighter and curled under just so.

"So how was your day?" he asked her.

"No classes today," she said. "Office hours. One of my students is working on his senior thesis, a collection of poetry, and it's just… oh, honey, it's just bad."

"Undergrad bad, or…?"

"No, like freshmen in high school, mopey, throw in a couple extra F-words for emphasis bad. He might be able to write mediocre Emo music."

"Needs a band?"

"And the ability to play an instrument or sing."

"Ouch."

"Yeah."

"Sorry," Joe said as he pulled a can of Pepsi out of the fridge.

"It's no big deal. We'll work on it. So, how about you?"

"Well, I hired a new guy today."

Christy turned away from the sink. "Really?"

"Yeah. He's a hard-core Duck. U of O stuff all over his car. Even a U of O pin on his computer bag. So that should be fun when it comes to Civil War time, with all the Beavers in the office."

Joe had attended Western Oregon University, the school where Christy now taught, so he wasn't particularly partisan when it came to Oregon's Civil War game, but he enjoyed the office trash talk. "The guy is young. So it's a mixed bag. On the one hand, he's hungry. I'm sure he plans on having my job in a year. On the other hand, he's got a lot to learn, so…."

"So he won't have your job in a year."

Joe smiled. "No."

"It's like our new guy, Luke."

Joe frowned as he sipped his soda, and Christy had to wait while he swallowed. "Who?"

"I told you about the new adjunct. Creative Writing and American Lit? Wants to write the next great American novel?"

"Oh yeah, I remember," Joe lied.

"Same thing. Young, ambitious." Christy didn't mention that he was also very handsome.

"Thinks he'll have your job in a year?"

"Well, I think he wants to publish a wildly successful book and leapfrog over me to some top-tier school." Christy also had a suspicion that Luke Devereaux wanted to leap onto her a bit before bounding off to his next destination, but she couldn't be sure if that was wishful thinking. She felt guilty, not because she was considering cheating, but just for wanting to be wanted by another man.

Of course she didn't say this. Which meant she didn't say anything. Which meant Joe felt like he was supposed to reply, and didn't know what to say.

"Yeah. Same thing," he said.

"Yeah."

Silence.

Joe sat and watched cartoons with Dawkins for a bit, then sat with his family for dinner (a chicken casserole dish with a side of reheated corn and rolls cut from a tube) in a room painted the lightest shade of blue he could find in both Magritte's "The Son of Man" and van Gogh's "The Starry Night." Magritte's apple-faced man and van Gogh's dizzying clouds listened quietly while Dawkins entertained his parents with the profound and tragic story of one of his classmates' misbehavior and subsequent punishment. The moral of the story seemed to be that a person could get away with a the use of a specific taboo word during morning recess and at lunch, but this could easily lull the careless miscreant into a false sense of security, and when he used the word in class during the afternoon he would meet swift and severe justice that would more than compensate for the lax security of the playground and cafeteria. Joe said the lesson should be that it's safest to avoid the word altogether, in order to prevent such slip-ups. Christy argued that it was important to learn that different language is appropriate in different settings, and asked Dawkins to imagine a circumstance where the term in question (Dawkins called it "The C word," by which he meant "crap") might be appropriate. Dawkins decided that he wouldn't feel comfortable calling his poop "crap" (though he found it hysterical that his mother had said "poop" at the dinner table), and chose to take his father's advice and avoid the word altogether, at least for the time being. Joe pronounced this a victory for Daddy over the insidious linguistic relativism of Mommy.

Christy daintily dabbed at the corners of her mouth with her napkin and spoke with patient dignity. "Yeah, just wait a few years until you hear some of the crap coming out of his mouth, and then we'll decide who has the more effective parenting strategy when it comes to language."

"Mom!" Dawkins shouted, shocked and delighted.

After the meal, Joe decided to watch the news. The room's eggshell white walls matched those in Raphael's "School of Athens," which hung above Joe's recliner. Plato and Aristotle could have seen the TV from their position, but chose to ignore it and carry on their animated discussion about forms and first causes. Considering the events discussed on the.TV, Joe thought that wise.

A pair of missiles had missed their targets and killed twelve civilians in Afghanistan.

A right-wing senator had taken a break from barking about fiscal responsibility to place a rolling hold on all judicial nominees in order to win some massive pork spending for his state.

Some bankers got big bonuses for driving their companies to the brink of bankruptcy.

A professor of neurobiology found out she wasn't getting tenure at her university, walked into a faculty meeting, and killed three of her colleagues. Turned out she'd shot and killed her brother 24 years earlier.

One former politician criticized the president for using a teleprompter while using notes she'd written on her hand. Another former politician criticized the president for not committing war crimes with the same vim and vigor he'd shown back when he was in office.

At that point Joe turned off the TV in disgust. His irritation was compounded by the fact that pinching the soft rubber button on the remote with all his might didn't make the screen snap to black any more dramatically. Nor did it somehow transmit his revulsion to the talking heads on the other side. Joe felt this was a design flaw, and that someone ought to create an app for it.

Noticing the time on the clock on the microwave, Joe called to Dawkins. "Bedtime!"

Bedtime was actually a long routine. It wasn't a shower night (every other for the seven-year-old), but Dawkins had to go to the bathroom, wash his hands and face, brush his teeth, drink some water, get into his pajamas, realize he had to pee again, and then settle in for his book. He was old enough to accomplish all the individual tasks on his own, but he needed Joe or Christy to check that each one had been completed. Joe and Christy didn't take regular turns, but lobbed the job back and forth depending on who had more evening work to accomplish. Tonight Christy had essays to grade, and Joe hadn't brought any paperwork home, so he took the gig.

Dawkins didn't care which parent served as his supervisor in the bedtime routine, but he knew that each parent read a different book to him, so his preference changed depending on which book he was enjoying most at the time. Currently, Joe was reading to him from The Chronicles of Narnia, a series Christy wouldn't touch with a ten-foot pole.

"Christian allegory? Really?" she'd asked.

"I liked it when I was his age. It is a lot of fun."

"Humph." This was the credo of Christy's devout atheism. She was reading Dawkins The Phantom Tollbooth, which, she felt, he didn't appreciate enough.

Dawkins curled up in his father's lap while Joe sat in his recliner. Joe read a passage about Aslan, and couldn't help but like the character. He made a mental note to ask Yahweh about the depiction of Aslan at their next weekly meeting. He instantly regretted even considering the idea. He actively tried to forget about the impending meetings as much as possible each week, and now it would hover at the bottom of his mental to-do list each day, like an itch he'd decided not to think about for fear of scratching it. What was that thing he needed to do? Oh yeah. Not think about the rash. Shit.

In that night's reading, Peter had to kill a wolf. Aslan could have done it for him, but he wanted Peter to prove himself, become a man, and prepare to be the High King. Joe held his son Dawkins close as he read this portion, not to comfort his scared son (Dawkins was loving the action, squirming with excitement) but to comfort himself. This scene rang particularly true. Joe thought it was a dick move on Aslan's part. What kind of super-lion puts children in danger (not just Peter, but his younger sisters, too) so one child can prove himself? And yet, even this was more laudable in Aslan than similar behavior from Yahweh, who would do something like that with even baser motivation. Peter was being prepped to be king. But what about Joe? He was being used as a sounding board. And what about Dawkins? Down unto the fourth generation. That was the rule.

Joe's chest tightened, whether from love for his son or from anguish at his own inability to protect Dawkins from his fate. Or was that despair turning into hatred? Or hatred into despair? Joe knew it only as an ache he couldn't quite name. He wrapped his large hand around Dawkins' ribs and pressed the boy's rib cage against his own, like a balm. It didn't work.

"What?" Dawkins asked, looking up at him.

"Do you think Aslan should have let Peter kill the wolf, or should he have done it himself?"

"It would have been cooler to see him do it."

Joe nodded. "I think so, too."

"I hope we get to see him do more fighting later."

"We will."

"But I like Peter, so it's good to see him win."

"I like Peter, so I want him to stay safe."

"But safe isn't cool, Dad," Dawkins said, rolling his eyes.

Joe gently bonked Dawkins' head with his own. "I guess you're right."

After Joe tucked Dawkins into bed, he came back down the stairs and found Christy turned in her chair, looking at him. "What was that about?"

"What?"

"Peter and Aslan."

"Oh, you heard that?"

"Yeah. Having second thoughts about your Jesus-Lion book?

"More like I'm having second thoughts about letting Dawkins get any older than, say, eight. At that point we just say, 'Nope. No more.'" He karate chopped the air. "'You're done.'"

Christy stood slowly, stepped over to her husband, and wrapped her arms around him, leaning her head on his shoulder. "Agreed. I mean, we can negotiate the exact year, but certainly not anything ending in –teen."

"Deal," Joe said, but he knew they weren't talking about the same thing. He felt a variation on the chest pain, and recognized some guilt straining a few of the muscles in the intercostal spaces between ribs five and six on his right side. But he could also feel Christy's breasts pressing on the left side, and he found this more than comforting.

The guilt came back during sex itself, which Joe found inconvenient. He tried to exorcise the emotion through added effort, and as they lay together afterwards, he could hear a smile in Christy's breathing. He knew that should have made him happy, but it only made the guilt worse.

Christy was pleased by the sex itself, but she was even more pleased that, in the heat of the moment, when Joe was really "on," she didn't once think of Luke Devereaux. She suspected her own ability to be genuine and in-the-moment had made it better for Joe. She didn't even notice that he didn't make eye contact as they crossed paths in the doorway of the bathroom.

Joe felt like the worst kind of liar, and he couldn't sleep.

5

Ghair Aadi looked out the window of his little apartment. Paris in the morning. He hated the view. He hated the filthy city and all its inhabitants. He even hated the gaudy church at the top of the hill. But, more than any of these, he hated the size of the little window. Why would the Parisians, living in a city that people paid so much to come visit, build such shitty little windows in their apartments? Stupid French.

The apartment was blessedly quiet. His roommates were already gone to their day jobs. He heard laughter from the street below. A group of American high school students hoofed it up his street, the Rue du Steinkerque, which led to the famous church, the Basilique du Sacre Coeur, at the top of the hill. The students would stand around, admiring the building or at least pretending to do so, and then they would walk down a few streets, past all the sex shops, to see the Moulin Rouge down on the Boulevard de Clichy. They held this cabaret theater in at least equally high esteem, and treated both with a kind of religious reverence. Ghair Aadi liked this about them. It seemed honest, or maybe it just matched his tastes. After all, the basilica was a beautiful architectural structure. He respected that. But the Rouge also carried quite a bit of history and cultural importance. Ghair Aadi found them equally holy.

In general, he liked Americans. For one thing, if he were driving a taxi in New York instead of Paris, he'd have a whole lot more room in his cab. With a medical degree, a thick accent, and no knowledge of the city's streets, he felt he was perfectly qualified to drive a cab there. Plus, the American racism toward Muslims and Arabs felt more muted than the vitriolic spite of the Parisians. Most Americans seemed to have the good sense to keep their racism private, and to make a show of looking down their noses at lower class people who voiced the same things they privately felt. Ghair Aadi thought this was a kind of progress. What had Martin Luther King said about law? It couldn't make a man love him, but it could keep a man from lynching him, and he thought that was pretty important. Ghair Aadi felt that way about shame. It couldn't make a man treat him as an equal, but it might keep someone from spitting in his face or shouting a slur as he passed by, and he thought that would be a nice change of pace. The world needed a lot more of it.

As he watched the students pass by, he wondered about them. Where were they from? A small town, like he was?

Perhaps some of them didn't feel accepted back home. Hell, they were teenagers. None of them felt accepted, even when they were alone. He thought he might have been able to make a life for himself in America, if things had worked out differently.

Then he wondered how many of these kids he would kill. Would they see his face on their televisions before they died? Here they were, walking up a street in Paris, and the man who would possibly kill them, and certainly appear in a jihadi video on every TV in their country, was looking down on them almost lovingly.

As Ghair Aadi turned and headed back into his kitchen to make himself some tea, he hummed the tune to "It's a Small World After All."

He grabbed the box of tea off the top of the fridge. As much as his roommates drove him crazy, at least they never touched his tea. They didn't like Persian tea. They wanted the tea from their own countries, and though they'd share with one another, they left his alone. If only they'd be as respectful of his food in the fridge, his books, the mess in the living room, the sink full of dishes. They accepted him as a fellow Sunni, but he would never be truly one of them. Deep down they all suspected that, because he was Persian and not an Arab, he was a secret Shiite.

If only they knew, one of the voices in his head said.

They'd never believe it if you told them, another said.

Shut up, he thought.

Ghair Aadi didn't find the voices shocking. They'd been regular companions since his days in university. He was no fool. He knew, even back then, what that meant. In his mid-twenties, when he'd started to hear them, he'd diagnosed himself right away. Schizophrenic. Essentially untreatable. He'd read the literature. He considered taking medication. He decided against it. As long as he could function, he could live with the voices, he'd decided. Besides, they were helpful sometimes. Ghair Aadi couldn't be sure if they'd come up with the plan, or if they'd only helped him flesh it out, but what difference did it make? They were, after all, just constructs of his broken mind. But the plan was sound. The plan was the rope he held on to.

After medical school in Saudi Arabia, he'd begun his post-graduate work in bio-engineering. With those kinds of credentials, it hadn't been hard to find an extreme fundamentalist Imam interested in helping him with his Islamic education. He'd studied furiously, feverishly. He memorized most of the Quran, reminded by the voices in his head when he forgot a passage. It was all part of the plan.

Then, one day, his Imam told him to go and meet with some people. He was taken through the kitchen of a small restaurant to a back room, where a man came in.

"Do you know who I am?" the man had asked.

"No, sir."

"That's fine. I'm not important. I am a soldier, committed to Jihad, just like you."

Ghair Aadi looked quickly at the other men standing around the room. The man in front of him was not a common soldier. Ghair Aadi hoped he was high enough in al Qaeda to fit into his plan. He couldn't allow himself to be bogged down with the concerns of al-Qaeda in the Arabian Peninsula. He already had his target in mind.

"You are committed, aren't you?" the man asked.

"Yes, sir."

"Your accent. It's strange to me. Where are you from?"

"Iran, sir."

"But you are an Arab?"

"Yes, sir."

"And a Sunni?"

"Yes, sir."

"That is… not normal." Then he smiled. The other men, the ones with their hands tucked into their robes, fingers wrapped tightly around the handles of their pistols, laughed. Ghair Aadi smiled, too.

The man who claimed to be a normal Jihadi soldier sipped his tea. "I think you will be quite special to us. In fact, Not Normal, I think you may do amazing things for Allah. You may change the world. Would you like that?"

"I seek only to do Allah's will," he'd said. And that was that. He was accepted and given a new name: Ghair Aadi, Arabic for "Not Normal."

They told him they wanted him to do some specialized work for them. Biological weapons. He told them what he'd need. Supplies. Money. Documents. Cover. And he told them where he wanted to hit. He watched the man's reaction carefully, worried that the man had a much smaller vision, some local, petty squabble.

"You will have everything you require. We will communicate through the men we send to you. You and I will not speak again."

Ghair Aadi made sure he looked disappointed. He felt greatly relieved. The plan remained intact.

He'd moved into this crummy apartment here in Paris with a bunch of true believers. Each night they prayed together, read from jihadi websites, watched Al Jazeera, and railed against Israel and the West. Ghair Aadi worked part time as a cab driver. And he worked on his little project. His hobby. His little bugs. All part of the plan.

But he did not serve the will of Allah. Ghair Aadi did not believe Allah existed. Or the Christian God. Or the Hindu's Vishnu. Or any other god. He never had. He thought all believers were fools, dupes, suckers. Worse, they would kill for their delusions. He could ignore the voices in his head. He was a man of science. But when his little bugs did their marvelous work, the true believers would do the rest.

He turned on the gas stove and pushed the button. A tiny spark lit the range. Blue fire danced under the teapot.

The Christians would demand blood, and their politicians would give it to them. The Muslims would fight back, smashing themselves like waves against the stone cliffs of the largest military in human history. Meanwhile, people would keep on getting sick. The world would be cleansed of its false gods, one way or another.

The videos, one of the voices said.

Those are the keys, another said.

"I know. I know. I'll get to them soon," Ghair Aadi said to the empty apartment.

We're not nagging, the first voice said.

Just helping, like a to-do list, the other said.

"You're nagging. I'll get them done. We're on schedule."

Okay. Just don't forget.

The bells in the Basilica rang for the eight o'clock morning mass. Ghair Aadi washed his teacup, dried it, and set it back in the cupboard, while sneering at his roommates' dishes in the sink. Then he washed his hands carefully, preparing for the morning's work in his bedroom lab.

"I don't forget things," he told the voices. "You don't let me."

You can't afford to, the first voice said. It's not an easy task, killing God.

Heck no, the second said. Golly, it's hard work.

6

On the top floor of the Valhalla corporate headquarters, Yahweh sat in His leather chair, His back turned on His empty desk. A cluttered desk was a sign of middle management, in His opinion. God's desk was wide and made of stone, perfect for sacrificing large livestock but impractical for paperwork. He rested an elbow on the rough surface while He stared out the window, over The City, into the void beyond. He felt nostalgic for the void. It hadn't been so bad.

Gabriel opened the door to the office, then knocked. "Sir?"

Yahweh turned slowly. "Is it time?"

"Yessir."

"Shit. I feel like I just sat down." He leaned forward slowly, grunting like a tennis player in slow motion, then rose and floated just above the floor, his body all straight lines pointing up to his oversized shoulders.

"Conference Room D, sir."

"Lead the way."

As Gabriel walked down the hall, God floated just behind him and asked, "So, did you get me any names of Inanna's newest associates?"

"It seems she's been busy, as usual. Most of the chatter is about her, um, involvement with both Ekkeko and Horus."

"She's banging both?"

"Yessir."

"I thought she'd had a falling out with Horus."

"It seems they've patched things up. But her bedroom companions are the least interesting of her friends. She's been spending quite a bit of time with Enlil and someone who hasn't been around for a while."

"Who's that?"

"Her name is Chalchiuhtotoliq. She goes by-"

"Toliq. Yes, I remember her. 'Precious Night Turkey.' Aztec goddess of pestilence and mystery. If I remember correctly, she's a moron, right?"

Gabriel nodded. "I always thought so, sir."

"So what use is she to Inanna?"

"Maybe she keeps her around to piss off her husband. Your son has little patience for the holier-than-thou types, especially if they're idiots."

"Takes after his old man in that regard," Yahweh said.

Gabriel smiled. "Well, he has little patience. You have no patience."

"True. So that's the question, then. Is she using Toliq to bug Jesus so she can keep on whoring it up with these other guys, or is she really trying to annoy me?"

They'd arrived at the door to the room. Gabriel opened it. "Good question, sir."

No one sat around the conference table, but the room felt half full as various gods stood around talking, mostly by a side table with coffee, donut holes, and Danish. As Yahweh passed through the room he said hello to a few of the gods. He picked the ones he could fairly assume to be on his side. He complimented Ixtab (Maya goddess of suicide and current goddess of journalism) on her lace gown and her wide headdress made of black feathers. He casually knocked elbows with Ogoun (Yoruban and Haitian god of craftsmen and modern god of the working poor). Meme (the god of atheism) sneered at Him, Yahweh growled back, and they both smiled at their inside joke. Then God shook hands with Agni (Hindu god of fire and modern god of science) at the breakfast table, before grabbing a glazed donut hole and popping it in his mouth.

His mouth still full, He said, "So, I understand Inanna has a presentation for us today? Very exciting. Let's get started." He rounded the table and sat at the head.

The other gods found their seats.

Inanna, who'd been hanging out in the hallway, made her entrance with Toliq and Enlil in tow. Inanna, though currently the goddess of The Church and Yahweh's daughter-in-law, was a former Sumerian fertility goddess and came in looking the part, her lips just slightly too large, too red, too wet, her breasts threatening to pop out of her severe suit coat and tight blouse, and her short skirt and fuck-me pumps promising a bountiful

47

harvest. Chalchiuhtotoliq had apparently been taking fashion tips from her new friend, though she wore trendy, thick-rimmed glasses and a suit coat of a particular shade of fuchsia sure to remind everyone she could give them the pox. Enlil, currently the god of American political discourse, wore wild eyes under insanely bushy eyebrows. His hair was feathered and styled just so, and his gait more than a bit fey as he walked in, but the tilt of his head was all whispering rage. Yahweh tried to remember if he'd looked the same back when he'd worked as the Sumerian god of air.

Between the former god of air and the "Precious Night Turkey," two ghosts in shackles and handcuffs came clinking and dragging into the conference room. The gods at the table looked at one another, and Yahweh was pleased to find he could still be surprised, if only by the surprise of the other gods who stifled gasps. The dead weren't particularly forbidden within the corporate Valhalla office building, but since they served little purpose to the living or the immortals they weren't ever brought in. Beyond that, putting them in chains seemed ridiculous. The City and its surrounding countryside were neither places of punishment nor reward for the dead. The afterlife served no moral function. So why bother to manacle two pathetic-looking ghosts?

Inanna pretended to speak directly to God as she addressed the whole room. "Yahweh, I want to thank you, first of all, for your willingness to indulge this little presentation. I hope it amuses you."

Sure you do, bitch, God thought, but He only smiled and nodded for her to proceed.

"We've had a fun little coincidence, and I wanted to share it with you. We had a couple of new arrivals show up. Within a period of just a few months, both these men died. They really want to see you, sir. And I think we would all be entertained to see their reaction upon finally meeting you."

Inanna stepped to the side and motioned to the two men like a game show hostess displaying the solved puzzle or the washer and dryer set. The two men shuffled forward, past Toliq and Enlil, and stood at the end of the table, across from Yahweh. They looked up at him for a moment, a bit sheepish, then looked back at the ground.

"Go on," Yahweh said to Inanna.

"These two men are the ghosts of Abdullah Asieri and Oral Roberts, your most Holiest of Holies."

God frowned.

Inanna smiled, "I thought you might be willing to tell us which of them you like better."

Shit, Yahweh thought.

The two men looked up again. They both realized Yahweh was looking at them and that Inanna had been addressing Him. Then both fell down on the floor, their faces pressed to the carpet. Chains rattled as Abdullah Asieri made a desperate effort to remove his sandals. Oral Roberts caught this out of the corner of his eye and made an equally vigorous effort to kick off his patent leather wingtips before the pagan next to him.

"Oh God-the-Father-Almighty," the ghost of Oral Roberts bleated, "I served you mah whole life just so I could hear you say 'Well done, mah good an faithful servant.' And here I am. Praise Jesus!"

"Allah, His... I mean, Your name be praised," the ghost of Abdullah Asieri said, "I have martyred myself for Your sake. Accept me as Your humble servant forever!"

"Guys, guys…" God said.

"Praise Jesus!"

"Praise Allah and his prophet Muhammad!"

"No, praise Jesus!"

"Allah!"

While the men cried out their slogans, they started banging their shoulders into one another in a pathetic re-enactment of the Crusades.

Yahweh got fed up. "Silence." He didn't sound like He was shouting, but the sound of His voice blew out the windows in the room and shook the whole building. Dust fell from the ceiling and made the only sound in the room as it sprinkled on the conference table.

God closed his eyes, frowned, and inhaled slowly through his nose. The window glass floated back into place, and the dust rose back up into the rafters.

Once He'd finished the repairs and calmed Himself, God spoke. "Guys, you're not going to like hearing this, but you're talking to the wrong god. Mr. Roberts, you haven't been working for me. You served this fellow here." Yahweh motioned down the conference table with an open hand. "This is Daikokuten. That's what the Japanese called him, anyway. The Incas called him Ekkeko, and we prefer that, because it's shorter. He's the god of wealth. You called him Prosperity, and you preached his gospel."

Ekkeko smiled at Roberts and waved. "Well done, my good and faithful servant." The gods around the table all chuckled. Even Yahweh smiled.

"And Mr. Asieri…well, I'm not sure who exactly you have been serving. Maybe you wanted to serve Ogoun, here. He's the god of workers and the poor." Ogoun scratched his bushy mustache and shook his head. "Or maybe you were serving Hel, the goddess of the dead, though I doubt it. Maybe you were manipulated by Horus there, the god of politicians and kings. How about it, Horus? Was this guy a political tool of yours?"

Horus shook his head. "A tool, sure. But not mine."

"Mr. Asieri, I think you're going to get this kind of rejection a lot, here. And do you know why?"

"Why, Lord?" Abdullah said into the carpet.

"Because you shoved explosives up your ass in an effort to blow up a Saudi prince."

"He was an infidel, Lord. An instrument of the West, the Great Satan, your enemy."

God ignored this. "Up your ass. You know, the living call you 'the butt bomber.' I don't think any god is going to want to shake your hand for that."

"There is no god but Allah. If you are not Him, you are all Djin, demons sent to torment me by Satan."

"You mean the Great Satan, America? So now we're what, CIA agents?" Yahweh looked around the table. "Well, ladies and gentlemen, I guess we've been promoted."

Everyone laughed. But then, they had to.

"Oh, Lord!" Roberts shouted. Cutting off the laughter irritated the gods, and everyone scowled at him. "Lord, my only wish was to serve you. Please, my God, be merciful. Forgive this sinner! I—"

"Turn down the volume, Roberts," Yahweh ordered. "Your show is over. No one needs to believe in your shtick anymore. There are no old ladies who will call and give you money here. There might be a few looking to give you a good kick in the family jewels, though." He sighed. Then he shook his head in irritation, as though waking up to some unpleasant realization. "And why are you still talking to me. I thought I made myself clear. You served Ekkeko. If you're looking for some kind of reward in the afterlife, ask him. And good luck, because the god of wealth is notoriously stingy. Personally, I always liked siding with the poor. Not because they're better or necessarily deserving. I just think rich people are arrogant, and their pride bothers me. But my son, he loves poor people. If I give somebody a horrible disease, he wants to heal them. If they take up the world's oldest profession, he'll sit down and have a meal with them. You know how much of a person's wealth should be given to the poor, according to my son? All of it. Yep. All of it."

"But Paul said to tithe—"

"Paul was a man, you idiot," God said. "One minute he was being manipulated by Jesus. The next minute by Horus over here. He's the god of kings and politicians. Inanna had her claws in him, too." He turned to his daughter-in-law. "No offense, dear."

She fashioned her nails into dangerous looking claws, made a dramatic pawing gesture, then winked at Yahweh. "None taken."

The wink was a mistake. Yahweh had been on a roll, and He'd lost sight of the trap Inanna had been trying to lay for Him, but that wink, that inherently inclusive expression, reminded Him that she was His enemy, and woke Him to the danger of the moment. He realized she was taking a stab at one of His weaknesses, His pleasure at hearing Himself speak. It's one thing to enjoy one's own voice, especially if one can speak a universe or two into existence, but it's quite another to revel so much in the sound that intelligence and foolishness trade places and the voice itself becomes an instrument for one's enemies. Yahweh made a mental note to say that to Joe at coffee next week; it would sound good to hear it spoken aloud, but He had to wait for the right time and place to say it.

Carefully, Yahweh closed his eyes, took a slow breath, then looked at Roberts. "Why am I explaining Myself to you? I am under no obligation. That's one of the things humans so rarely understand. Extort millions from people by telling them it's good to be thrifty, or shove some plastique up your ass along with a cell phone and give yourself one last call. Either way, it doesn't buy you anything from Me. I'm not your stock-broker, your fortune teller, your drug dealer, your am radio blowhard, or your UPS delivery guy. I don't owe you anything. I made you, and that was quite a bit more than either of you two deserved." He turned to Inanna. "So, Inanna, I'll answer your question. Which of these two do I like better? When I made the Leviathan, how far down in the sea was he? And when I cast down the angels, how far, exactly, did they fall? Oh, that's right. You weren't there. So if I were to say these two are both beneath my contempt, how far down does my contempt go, Inanna?"

"'Surely I spoke of things I did not understand, things too wonderful for me to know,'" she quoted. "I apologize if I have offended you, Lord and Father."

Sure you do, you bitch, Yahweh thought.

He smiled. "Well, it was a valiant attempt anyway, Inanna. I am not easy to amuse."

She tried to hide her rage, but the tops of her ears turned the same shade of red as her friend Toliq's sport coat. Toliq herself looked from side to side in confusion, but she wore the same plastered-on smile as always.

"I have a lunch meeting to attend. If there's no business more pressing than…," he waved a hand at Roberts and Asieri, "Prosperity Pimp and Proctologist's Nightmare here, I'll excuse Myself a bit early today."

The gods at the conference table all nodded and began gathering their papers and talking with the divinities to their right and left. Yahweh rose and walked out of the boardroom, and as he passed Inanna he patted her on the shoulder.

As he walked down the hall, he turned to Gabriel who followed close behind him. "So, lunch with Frigga?"

"And Isis and Osiris, at Dante's."

"Right. Hey, just between you and me," Yahweh said, as the elevator doors closed, "for the record, I think I prefer Asieri. He's more amusing. I'll bet he listened to a preacher who didn't have the courage to shove explosives up his own butt. The most that Roberts ever did for Me was pluck his eyebrows and bleach his teeth."

7

Christy, saying goodbye to a student, stepped backward out of the doorway to the classroom in the education building and nearly bumped into Luke Devereaux, who was coming out of his own room into the foyer.

"Oh, sorry," she said, catching the stack of books and manila envelopes falling out of her arms.

He reached out to catch them as well, but she leaned back and they all fell into place.

"Headed back to the office?" he asked.

"Yeah. Just finished Renaissance Brit Lit."

Devereaux pointed a thumb over his shoulder. "Fiction Workshop."

"Oh, how's that going?"

"Some gems, some diamonds in the rough, some rocks, some dirt."

Christy nodded. "Do you have…," She lowered her voice and stepped toward the building's front doors, motioning for him to follow with her head since her hands were full. "…Kyle Thompson?" she whispered. She knew he did.

Luke rolled his eyes the slightest bit. "Yeah." He sighed.

"He's one of my advisees. I've seen his senior project."

Luke sucked a breath in through his teeth. "Yeah."

"I know! What are we going to do?"

The classes had been held in the education building, which was built on the back side of a sloping hill. They had to walk up half a flight of stairs to a landing between the first and second floors in order to exit the building under a covered walk that connected to the computer science building next to it on the main drag. They walked along the short path toward North Monmouth Avenue, the street that ran through the center of campus. Students filed past and cluttered the sidewalk in front of them, making them both self-conscious about the volume of their conversation. "I wish I had an easy answer to the question of Kyle," Luke said. "I mean, the big question is what to do about bad writers who suffer from anosognosia."

"What's that?"

"The condition in which someone who suffers from a disability doesn't know they have the disability, or denies its existence. In extreme cases people lose a limb or go blind and say the limb is still there, or that they can see. Bad writers refuse to acknowledge that they are just bad at it."

"Well, that will be my word for the day, then. Anosognosia," she repeated.

"A very sad condition. And severe, in Kyle's case."

"I told my husband the kid could write bad lyrics for an Emo band, if he could sing or play an instrument." Christy felt a hitch in her voice when she mentioned Joe. Had she brought up her husband to ward off unwanted advances? To protect herself? Was it accidental, and did she now regret it? She didn't know where the feeling in her stomach came from.

"You want to add bad singing and bad music to his bad poetry? Ouch. Let's just get him a diploma and a job as an accountant or an insurance salesman or something. He can submit his poetry to the Polk County Fair and hopefully only one person will have to read it per year."

"Right," Christy said, but as they turned onto the sidewalk, she looked down at the pavement, suddenly deeply ashamed of her husband's profession. If Luke ever met Joe, and Joe told him he sold insurance, would Luke remember this conversation? Would he feel uncomfortable? Would she?

Christy and Luke crossed the street at the crosswalk leading to the Neil W. Werner University Center, the school's social hub housing the café, bookstore, etc. Instead of continuing that way, they followed the direction of Monmouth Avenue, crossing Church Street toward their offices. All the buildings were built out of nearly matching red brick to hide the layers of construction, formed like geological strata as the school evolved like sedimentary rock, pushing down eras one after another, the Oregon State Normal School, the Oregon Normal School, the Oregon College of Education, and Western

Oregon State College all buried under the weight of university status.

Trees, two or three stories tall, wore thick layers of moss on the bottom-most branches, like thin old ladies in fancy coats with giant collars of fur under even larger permed hairdos. Despite the similar bricks, the architectural styles of the buildings varied from the modern blocky buildings to vaguely Tudor to almost-Victorian and back to brick-covered-sixties-urban-housing-project. The trees did the aesthetic heavy lifting, tying it all together and making it feel simultaneously quaint and formally academic. And all, remarkably, without the slightest hint of ivy hanging onto any brick as far as the eye could see. As she walked along with Luke, Christy didn't know if she felt embarrassed by the look of the campus, or proud of its lack of pretension.

Christy glanced at Luke. She noticed the stubble on his face. She hated it when Joe's face got prickly. Why didn't Luke's stubble bother her? Joe didn't have that cleft in his chin, either. Or those heavy eyebrows. Or those light-brown, almost golden eyes.

She looked back at the ground in front of her. The papers in one of the folders started to slide, and she tried to corral them with her shoulders.

"Can I help you carry all that?" Luke asked.

"No, I've got it," she said too quickly. "I mean, we'd just drop it in the exchange and make a big mess."

"Probably."

They walked in silence for a moment.

An oversized truck, red, lowered, and too shiny for its own good, came hauling up the street behind them, rumbling as it passed. Though it was probably only exceeding the 20-mile-per-hour limit by a bit, when it hit the wide speed bump just ahead of them, it popped up and came down hard on the asphalt, scraping metal fingers on stone chalkboards.

"Oh, ouch." Luke laughed.

"What a... jerk," Christy said. Jerk? she thought. What the hell is wrong with me? Asshole. I meant asshole.

When she'd been in college, Christy had enjoyed telling people she "had to piss like a racehorse." Now she'd occasionally catch herself telling Joe she had to "potty," even when Dawkins wasn't within earshot. Once upon a time, she'd only used "cute" as the most cutting, bitter criticism. Now she called things cute all the time, and not just to describe the earrings of a colleagues or a friend's blouse, but to sum up her opinion on a movie she actually liked. "Funny" had become "silly". And "asshole" had become "jerk".

And now she was staring at the ground like a 14-year-old walking to her locker with the captain of the football team.

What had happened to her?

Did she really have a crush on the handsome young Ph.D. candidate? The cliché was nauseating.

Was she really contemplating cheating on her husband just to shake herself out of the ennui that comes from matrimonial bliss? If that were the plot of some terrible Lifetime movie, she'd change the channel.

Did she really believe some dirty one-night stand would magically make her a 19-year-old with an attitude again?

And how could he just walk next to her so quietly? Was he that confident? Or was he nervous in her presence, too?

"So," she interrupted herself, "are you going to the faculty get-together at the Bhatnagars'?"

"I'm not sure. Are those the kind of things adjuncts go to? I don't want to be a third wheel."

"Oh yeah, no, lots of adjuncts come. They bring their spouses. It's good to have new blood in the mix with all us stale old fogies."

"So you're going?"

"Yeah, I'm planning on it."

"Most of the English department folks will be there?"

"Yeah. Come to think of it, it is mostly humanities. Raktim Bhatnagar teaches math. There are some of the other math guys, too, but not too many science folks, over all. But, you know, good connections. Everybody in the room knows somebody somewhere else who might be looking for an English professor, so, it'd be a good career move to get to know as many people as possible."

"True. Is it all business?"

"No, not at all. Very informal and fun. But that's the best kind of business networking, right? Nobody likes the guy who is obvious about an agenda."

"Even though everybody has an agenda."

"Exactly."

"Sounds like something out of Chekov or Wilde."

"Well, not that clever or that…wild. Pardon the pun. Not that Wilde is that wild. But you know, so much simmering under the surface. This isn't like that. Pretty tame, but fun."

Luke almost laughed. "Well, if you say it's safe, I guess I'll have to go."

"I guess I don't advertise for it too well, but it really is fun."

"Okay." He smiled at her. She found it oppressive, like the waves of heat that rolled on the streets on a summer day.

They both looked both ways before crossing the street.

Neither spoke as they made their way down the sidewalk toward Belamy Hall, the Humanities/Social Science Building, known to students as the HSS, where the English Department had its offices. The two story block of brick was decorated only with some tall windows above the main doors, but it stood so close to Campbell Hall, which housed the Art Department, that the two buildings could be mistaken for one. Campbell looked like a large, pretty brick church, the kind that might be found in Topeka, Kansas or Champaign, Illinois. The two together looked like a Midwestern Protestant's version of a cathedral, all brick and white-trimmed windows and nothing too bold, lest it be mistaken for Catholic. Christy's office was upstairs, high in the humble cathedral's nave, and Luke's was on the first floor, near its crossing.

They slowed almost imperceptibly in the HSS foyer.

"So, I'll see you there," Christy said. I'll see him a dozen times before that, she thought. Dammit!

"Um, yeah, okay, I'll go."

"Great. I mean, good." Dammit, she thought again. I sound like an idiotic girl.

Inside her office, she tried to set the pile on the corner of her desk. The tower leaned, slid, then fell on the floor.

She let herself fall into the chair she kept for students, sighed, and began picking up the papers. She picked up a sheet that had made a longer leap than the rest. Kyle Thompson's name was printed in the upper right-hand corner, and the poem was neatly left-aligned, except for the last line, which stood off by one standard indentation. He'd used different fonts, italics, and underlining to make up for the words themselves. The last lines read:

"Trapped in the chains of monogamy
Wrapped *around my neck,* strangling
Passion **breaks** free
Ejaculate for FREEDOM
But **LOVE** is a DOUBLE EDGED-SWORD
screaming
Fuck this shit!!!"

Christy closed her eyes and let the poem fall into her lap. So awful! If Kyle Thompson could speak to the secrets of her soul, she was in deep trouble.

8

Jesus scratched his belly absently, and found a fragment of a sour-cream-and-onion Pringle lodged in his bellybutton. About two inches of his gut was sticking out below his shirt, and the crumbs of his chips had formed a layer of rough sediment there. Jesus wasn't particularly fat, though he'd allowed himself to lose the toned physique he'd maintained back in his carpentry days. It wasn't his fault. He hadn't had much to do for at least, what? Seventeen hundred years? Eighteen? Plus, they didn't have Pringles in Palestine during the Roman occupation. Once Jesus had popped, he couldn't stop.

Jesus took the crumb in his bellybutton as a sign, stood up, and brushed the chips off his stomach onto the shag carpet.

He'd kept the orange and brown shag when his dad had the rest of the house re-carpeted to keep up with the style. Jesus liked shag. It hid stains fairly well and felt comforting. Stainproof carpeting was a terrible invention, in Jesus' opinion. It made a person feel obligated to clean up the stuff magically floating on top. Jesus wanted it all to grind in and hide. That was how he felt about a lot of things, lately. Lately being the last couple millennia.

He noticed that the Pringles had also left dark little stains on his gray sweatpants, and near the bottom of his Queen t-shirt. The mottled gray of the sweats hid the stains better than the faded black of the shirt, and he thought about changing before going out. Oh, who cared? He wasn't trying to impress anybody.

Jesus stretched, groaned as he reached down to get the remote off the wagon-wheel coffee table, and aimed it at the TV. He hated that Maury Povich had gone to all-paternity-testing all-the-time. Jesus knew who the fathers were, but he couldn't help watch the mothers' reactions when they heard the news. Regardless of the outcome, he felt so badly for them. Even when the tests revealed the baby-daddy they preferred, Jesus would watch the woman look at the prospective mate's expression, hoping he'd be happy to find out the news. Jesus could empathize with her hope and terror in that moment. He could also sense the audience's disappointment. They wanted tears, screams of denial, dramatic storming offstage followed by a jiggling handy cam. Instead, they "ah"-ed reluctantly, and Jesus could see the fleeting relief twist into jaded judgment; she still didn't know which one was her baby-daddy, so she's a bad person.

This particular girl would escape that judgment, Jesus knew. Maury was about to tell her that the father wasn't her current boyfriend, or the one before that, but the one-night stand Maury had hidden backstage. Povich stretched out the pathos of the opening of the envelope as long as he could, then read the name. The woman mouthed "No, uh-uh," before slapping both hands in front of her face and screaming.

"We've brought him here. Would you like to see him?" Maury asked.

"No!" she screamed. Then she ran off the stage and nearly smacked into the man she didn't want to see. The cameraman with the handy-cam chased after her, then turned around them as the mother-to-be sank to her knees, screaming. Despite his best efforts, the cameraman couldn't avoid glimpses of her generous ass-crack poking up through the orange spandex shorts, and the tattoo of a Chinese symbol on her lower back. She thought is said "Pride," but Jesus knew it said "General Tso's Chicken".

The soon-to-be father tried his best to speak to the woman kneeling at his feet. Jesus watched the tender, awkward way he put a hand on her shoulder without any effect. Jesus felt some solidarity. Then the man looked right into the camera, shrugged, and smiled.

Hard cut to Maury, still sitting on stage next to Cheyenne's empty chair. "We'll be right back with Ronnie and Cheyenne, so don't go anywhere," Maury said. He sounded excited, but Jesus could tell Maury was bored.

Then the screen flicked to an image of a large, curvy, gentle "A" and "L" followed by a smaller, sharper "T" and "V." A woman's soft voice said, "You're watching the After Lifetime Television network. Pass the time with us."

It cut to a commercial for a service wherein angels would hand deliver mint juleps to your front porch and bill your credit card. Mint juleps were all the rage, as it had been unusually warm that summer in Hel.

Jesus pulled up the digital guide and flipped past the Afterlife News Network (motto: "Heaven's Perspective on Earthly Events. Great Distance=Less Bias."). That channel was strictly for the recently deceased. It was something of a joke in heaven. How could you identify a Newbie? They still watched ANN. Since the dead couldn't interact with the living, and since the events of the living had so little impact on the dead (rates of immigration— that was about it) it really didn't matter to PLPs (post-living-persons). Of course, Jesus did care about the folks down there, but their intrigues only bummed him out. He had the ability to go down there whenever he wished, but he hadn't been in a while. He didn't enjoy playing a superhero, rescuing people from overturned cars or burning buildings, and he'd seen what happened whenever some likeness of his face appeared in the lichen on a rock or the burn marks on a grilled cheese sandwich; he didn't want to imagine what would happen if someone took a picture of him with their cell phone camera.

Jesus turned the TV off and set the remote back on the coffee table. He thought about taking another nap. He napped often, as a consequence of the depression. As he wandered back toward his bedroom, he caught sight of himself in the bathroom mirror. His black beard was getting a bit long, and his hair, parted in the middle, quickly turned into large black ringlets and hung almost to his shoulders. His sympathetic eyes identified him, though. Yeah, someone would still recognize him, Queen t-shirt and all, and take a picture. Nope. It wasn't safe to go down there.

In his room, he sat on the unmade bed but couldn't work up the energy to lie down. He looked at his closet and decided to change shirts. He pulled the Queen t-shirt off and threw it over his shoulder in the general direction of the hamper, then stood and flipped through the clothes hanging on the bar in the closet. He found a black t-shirt advertising the Jimi Hendrix experience, showing Jimi down on his knees, guitar on his lap, head thrown back, afro compressed by a tie-dyed headband. Jesus liked that image, but the look on Jimi's face was so rapturous Jesus just couldn't bring himself to put Jimi on his chest. Instead, he found a light blue t-shirt with a stylized "S" above the name Spacehog. That fit better. A defunct band from a bygone era set against a faded, dull background.

Jesus decided he needed a change of pace. For one thing, if he left his basement apartment, his step-mother would have some angels clean the room. It needed it. The laundry pile was just beginning to radiate a unique Shroud-of-Turin-meets-heavy-metal-fan kind of funk. Also, if he got out, he might feel up to wearing Jimi.

Rather than take one of his father's cars (Yahweh had a thing for impressive works of human engineering), Jesus chose to float over to a friend's house. When he got there, his friend wasn't home, so he went out looking for him. He found the former prophet Muhammad (peace be upon him) sitting in a particularly green field, watching over a flock of sheep and goats who were drinking from a stream below.

"Moe! How's it going?" Jesus said.

"Jesus. What's up, my friend?" Muhammad said.

"The usual. A whole lotta nothing."

Jesus sat down next to Muhammad and watched the goats and sheep. "They're thirsty," he said.

"I just brought them over from a hill about two kilometers that way. No reason. Good grass there. Grass in between. But I wanted to give them some exercise. And the creek is nice here."

"It is."

"Yep."

Mohammed let Jesus enjoy the sound of the creek and the color of the grass for a while. Finally he spoke.

"I'm glad to see you out of that basement." Muhammad turned and stared hard at Jesus. "I'm worried about you, man."

"Really? Nah, don't worry, Moe. I'm fine. You know, I let stuff get to me sometimes, but I'll get over it."

"So it's your wife again?"

"Inanna is…."

"See, I warned you."

"I knew what I was getting into. Or, I should have. I thought it made the most sense, for the sake of my apostles, to give them a competitive advantage. She had the structure in place. I thought I was co-opting the institutions, and…." He gestured for Muhammad to finish his sentence.

"…and the institution co-opted you. I had some experience with that, you know. The Meccans tried to do that to me. And the Medina clans, too." Muhammad fell silent for a moment, then shook his head violently and looked hard at Jesus. "No, you know what? I've got to say this. That's not even the full story, Jesus. Not by a long shot. She was a nice piece of ass, and you got played. And she's a slut. And you still love her, which is why she breaks your heart every time she bangs somebody else for political advantage."

Jesus bowed his head. "You're right."

"See, this is the problem with one wife. I was happily married to my first wife for 25 years. 25 years, my friend! But after she passed away, I married 12 more times. That's my advice. Dump Inanna. Sure, it would be a scandal for a while, but your father would support you in it completely. Then, find yourself a dozen other brides."

"You know I can't do that."

"So Inanna is the goddess of the Church Universal. So what? Go out and make someone the goddess of the Methodists, somebody for the Presbyterians. Take some nice Russian girl and make her the goddess of the Orthodox church. They don't like Inanna anyway."

"I don't know. Maybe. I'll think about it."

"No you won't," said Muhammad. "You'll go back to moping in the basement. You know I don't hold what your followers do against you, and I know you don't hold mine against me. And I respect that. I appreciate it. But what you do…Or don't do…. That is on you, my friend. I see what your wife has done to your church, and I am sorry for you. And I am angry for you. And when you don't do anything about it, I am mad at you. So don't say you'll think about it when you won't."

Jesus leaned away from Muhammad, stunned. He opened his eyes as wide as they'd go, blinked twice, and shook his head. Inhaling through his nose, he stood up. The goats and sheep looked up at him, not sure if they were safe in his presence.

"I will think about it. I am. We're basically separated now. I haven't lived with her in, what, three hundred years? The question is, would she get all of Christianity in the divorce?"

Jesus scratched his beard just beneath his bottom lip, felt something oily, tasted the hair and identified some leftover peanut butter.

Muhammad stood slowly and stretched. "Would it make a practical difference, my friend? You've always been a bit too idealistic, in my opinion. I'm more of a pragmatist. Inanna runs the whole organization right now anyway. If you're not going to take it back, then let it go. Why own it in name only?"

"Good point."

"And you need a bath. I've smelled goat dung with a more pleasant aroma."

Jesus smiled.

"See?" Muhammad said. "A smile! Get yourself someone who makes you smile, like a new wife. Or a project that makes you smile. Your father, he used to like making water come out of rocks in the desert for thirsty people to drink. That was one of his favorites. It made him smile. Make yourself smile more. Eternity is a long time to be unhappy."

Jesus nodded. "Thanks, Moe. I love you, man."

"Yeah, yeah." Muhammad put a heavy hand on Jesus shoulder and smiled. "You love everybody. Now go home and take a bath."

Muhammad walked down toward his flock. Jesus let his smile fade, but there was a new look in his eye. It wasn't a plan. Not yet. But for the first time in centuries, Jesus had an idea.

9

Dawkins ran across the backyard swinging a small stick. "Expelliarmus!" he shouted. "That one makes the wand fall out of your hand."

His friend, Bill E., dropped his stick as though it were on fire. Bill E. was one of two boys named William in their class, and for a few days William Johnston had been Bill J. to William Edwards' Bill E., but the second graders decided that Bill E. and Bill were distinct enough. Though Marcos and Darius climbed over one another for second place in Dawkins' rankings, Bill E. was Dawkins' most consistent Best Friend.

"What do I do now?" Bill E. asked, looking down at his wand.

"Dodge or I'll get you," Dawkins said.

Bill E. beamed. "Okay!" Then he began jumping from side to side, sometimes rolling in the grass, while Dawkins made explosion noises and yanked back on his stick as though propelled by the recoil of his spells.

"Dis-incinerato!" Dawkins yelled.

"What does that do?"

"It dis-incinerates you. You're blown up."

"Oh." Bill E. sounded a bit disappointed by this turn of events.

Dawkins sighed, rolled his eyes, and smiled. "Grab your wand," he told his magical arts student. "Let's try again."

"Okay. Let me dis-incinerate you this time!"

After all his rolling and dodging, Bill E. couldn't find his wand immediately. When his eyes fell on it, they lit up, and he ran toward it. Then he screamed.

"What? What?" Dawkins cried.

"Snake!"

Sure enough, there was a small, grayish-brown garter snake lying in the grass where the wand could have been.

Both boys screamed again and ran to the concrete slab by the sliding door. "What do we do?" Bill E. squealed.

"We have to get it."

"The snake?"

"No, your wand!"

Bill E. shook his head. "I'll get another stick."

"No, you need that one. Other sticks aren't as magic. You need the most magic one, and that was your wand. It's a Deadly Halo." (Joe had frequently corrected Dawkins' misinterpretation of Harry Potter's Deathly Hallows, but Dawkins liked the sound of Deadly Haloes better.)

"Uh-un." Billy E. shook his head from side to side as though he wanted his nose to fly off.

"I'll get it," Dawkins said. He walked boldly to the edge of the concrete pad, then hesitated to put a foot in the grass even though the snake was at least 15 feet away.

"Have courage, little warrior. Verily, this step may be the most difficult test of thine whole life."

Dawkins couldn't hear Thor next to him. He couldn't see the giant Norse god standing in the grass, arms crossed over his massive chest, blond hair flapping dramatically even though there was no wind to speak of. But somehow Dawkins felt a little shove of encouragement. He leaned out and let his foot fall into the snake-infested lawn.

"Thou hast done it!" Thor boomed, and Dawkins felt a rush of pride. He took another step. And another. Then he looked back at his best friend. Bill E. had made it to the edge of the porch, but wouldn't venture into the grass.

"Be not cowed by thy friend's hesitation," Thor advised. "Thou art now a leader of men. He will follow you if you are brave enough to challenge the serpent. Keep going, little warrior. Just a bit farther."

Dawkins tried to read his friend's expression, but Bill E.'s eyes, popped open as round as shiny quarters, could have been expressing awe at his bravery, or screaming out terror at the wand's capture, or calling Dawkins back from certain death. Dawkins couldn't tell.

He turned and took two more steps, acutely aware of Bill E.'s eyes on his back (and vaguely aware of Thor's gaze, too, though he couldn't identify the feeling). He scanned the grass in front of him but couldn't find the snake, and every time he convinced himself it remained just where he'd left it, he'd consider the possibility that the monster had slithered through the grass to sneak up on him. He scanned the lawn in front of his feet again. And again. Then he took another few steps before he stopped to examine every shady spot for a hint of scales.

"There is no shame in caution, little warrior," Thor said. "Bravery is measured in persistence, regardless of its speed. Keep going. Just a bit farther now."

Dawkins took one more step. Then he saw Bill E.'s wand. He ran to the stick, picked it up, and froze. Somewhere near his feet, he knew, the dragon slumbered. He spun in a slow circle and found it only a few feet from where he stood. He squealed but did not run.

"Thou knowest what thou must do," Thor said.

"What are you doing?" Bill E. shouted. "Run!"

But Dawkins couldn't. He lifted the stick over his shoulder and leaned toward the snake.

"Forbear, little warrior," Thor scolded. "Thou knowest the serpent is not thy true enemy. Thine enemy is thine own fear. Do not strike down the serpent. Thou knowest the course thine actions must take. Embrace thy fate. Conquer thy fear."

Dawkins couldn't hear Thor's words and probably wouldn't have been able to decipher the affected high speech. But he understood. He lowered the stick and bent down, crouching over the motionless garter snake. Then he reached out a shaky hand....

He touched the snake. It moved, but only a bit. Dawkins started, pulling his hand back, but he didn't fully stand. Then he reached out again and ran his fingers across the snake's back. The scales brushed the soft skin of his fingertips as the snake slipped away through the grass, then under the fence.

"I touched it!" Dawkins shouted, running back to Bill E. "I touched the snake!"

Thor inflated his broad chest, leaning back and looking down at the little boys, flashing his shiny teeth.

"And yet, you know they will die," Frigga said. It wasn't a question.

Thor turned away from the boys who bounced and danced on the little back porch. "Oh, greetings Mother." He dropped this high speech he liked to use to rally the troops. "How's it going?"

"I am well," she said.

"Good." He stood there, feeling uncomfortable in the silence, not knowing how to break it. His gaze returned to the celebrating boys. "He conquered his fear."

"And you love him for this." Frigga didn't ask questions very often. She knew the future perfectly. Back when she'd been married to Thor's father, she'd been the only other person allowed to sit on Odin's throne, Hliðskjálf, the magical high seat that allowed Odin to see into all realms at once. Not only had Frigga seen into all those dimensions, but she was also gifted with perfect prophecy. She never told what she knew, though. Thor had often wondered if she could see what would happen in alternate timelines where she shared her knowledge. Maybe they were worse and she refrained as a consequence. Or maybe the future she'd seen was so unchangeable that she just didn't want to bother. Either way, it strained their relationship. It's hard to talk with someone who knows everything you're ever going to say.

"I do love them. The courage of the mortals inspires me."

"It gives you courage as well," she said.

"Yes. Someday these boys will become aware of death. They will be tempted to lose hope. But maybe this boy here," he pointed at Dawkins, "will remember his courage, the courage he found today, and will march against fate until Hel takes him."

"And that gives you courage."

"Yes, Mother. Because I believe that I, too, will die one day. In the last battle, Dad will come out of the retirement home and be consumed by Fenrir. I will do battle with the World Serpent, Jörmungandr, no little garter snake but the monster that will destroy the World Tree that holds all the worlds together. I will defeat the serpent, but I will not long survive the battle. But my struggle will preserve the world, damaged though it will be, so that it can be renewed."

Frigga frowned, staring hard at her son. "You do not know that this will occur. This is what you believe."

"Well, sure. I have never sat upon Hliðskjálf, and I don't know the future the way you do, but this is my understanding of what is to come. I mean, it could all be allegorical, of course, but then, aren't we all? I try not to worry too much about such things. When a giant serpent big enough to destroy the universe is advancing and you have nothing but a magical hammer, the thought that both you and the serpent might only be characters in an epic poem isn't really very comforting." He looked at the boys again. "These boys, their triumphs…that is what comforts me."

Then he told Dawkins, "Go now, little warrior. Tell your mother the tale of your brave deed."

Dawkins eyes lit up as though he'd dawned upon the idea all by himself. He grabbed the sliding glass door, hauled on it with some difficulty, and shouted into the house for Christy. "Mom! Mom! I touched a snake!"

"What?" Christy called back, matching his excitement.

Thor listened to the boy's voice fade as the door slid closed. "I had to recue Bill E.'s wand from this snake, and I did, and I touched it!"

The door clicked shut, and Thor was left alone with his distant mother, greatest of the goddesses, all-knowing wife of Yahweh, ex-wife of Odin, mother of the universe. From his towering height, he looked down on her. She was beautiful, eternally young, eternally serene, as steady and distant at the Statue of Liberty seen from the fjords of Norway.

For the first time, Thor wondered if his desire to protect the mortals came as much from his love for their courage as from a kind of divine envy. Maybe he was jealous that they could boast of their deeds to mothers like Christy, and that those mothers were proud of their brave little boys. Those mothers had the capacity to love little warriors who would die someday. Did his?

"Well Mom, I've got to meet some guys at a thing we've got going on, so, um, I'm gonna take off, okay?"

Frigga stepped toward him, reached up, and gently placed her hand on his cheek. "I know," she said.

He unstrapped Mjölnir from his belt, leapt into the sky, and ascended to Asgard. And as he went, his eyes burned.

10

As she climaxed, Toliq's voice cried out toward the Paris sky. "Oh? Oooh? Oh, gosh! Oh my gosh!" Propped on her elbows, she let her head fall back and rest against the aluminum roof over Ghair Adi's apartment building. Her chest heaved as she caught her breath. "Wow," she whispered. "Golly."

Inanna popped up between Toliq's knees and looked down at her new partner's sprawled form. She enjoyed the way Toliq sounded surprised every time she came. Most of Inanna's other sexual partners weren't like that. Ekkeko, the god of wealth, liked it quick and dirty, and immediately after he finished he'd roll over and check his Blackberry. Horus, the god of politicians and kings, always had to be on top, and roared when he climaxed, then fell asleep right away. Enlil, the god of air and political discourse, loved to talk afterwards, and during, and before. Inanna had the feeling that the sex itself wasn't really as valuable to Enlil as the pillow talk, and because he was so…un-endowed, it wasn't really about the sex for her either. But Toliq, she was special.

When the Aztecs had called her Chalchiuhtotoliq ("Precious Night Turkey"), she was their goddess of pestilence and mystery. Since then, she'd staked out a new territory for herself as goddess of anti-intellectual fundamentalism. It wasn't a big stretch. She reveled in certainty in the face of contradicting facts, and greeted every new bit of information with a kind of wide-eyed, knee-jerk rejection. This annoyed Inanna sometimes. Toliq liked to try to insult people with labels she didn't understand, so that her tirades tended to devolve into gibberish. This gibberish was particularly disconcerting because it was always pitch perfect, like a virtuoso singing a melody, but with lyrics that had been cut out, tossed in a bag, shaken, and glued onto the sheet music in random order. Still, whenever Inanna would get tired of her, they could always have sex again. Toliq greeted her own sexuality with the same compulsive rejection she did everything else, not refusing to consent to the act, but refusing to believe she might enjoy it. Then, when she had sex with a Baalite fertility goddess, she greeted her own pleasure as something shocking and a bit unwelcome. Inanna loved that.

Inanna also realized how valuable Toliq was to her larger plans. She'd never be able to wrest control of the world away from Yahweh without a controlling interest in the world's people. Somehow, humans couldn't be entirely bought with money. She'd tried to align herself with Ekkeko, to join The

Church with wealth, and that hadn't done the trick by itself. She'd tried to marry The Church to the State, with the help of Horus, and that hadn't worked either. Even with those allies, she couldn't quite do it. She thought it was a PR problem, and used Enlil to spin her messages, but that hadn't worked, either. People wanted something else, something she couldn't give them with money and power and sex and the right sound bites.

And then she'd had a moment of inspiration. She didn't need to figure out how to give them what they wanted. She didn't even need to shape their desires. She just needed to make them so stupid they couldn't process their own longings into plans of any kind, and then she could dangle whatever she wanted in front of their blinking, open-mouthed faces and they'd follow her anywhere. Toliq could never do that on her own, but Inanna could. She could weave faith and money and sex together, then stain the whole thing in the color of nonsense. Then she could cast her quilt of despair over the sky, wrap up the planet in darkness, and steal it away from Yahweh. And what would He be able to offer? He was just a stupid builder. The people wouldn't be able to articulate any vision for the world they wanted to build. He'd be useless, dismissed like Zeus and Ra and Hadad to play bocce ball or shuffleboard and tell stories about their smiting days. And what would Inanna's husband, Jesus, be able to do about it, with his precious love? Maybe he could inspire people to write greeting cards. If his love couldn't keep his "children" from sending their own kids to go off and kill other kids, Inanna didn't give a flying fuck what it said on the folded pieces of paper they used to greet the bodies that came home.

The thought of Jesus crying over the humans in his basement made Inanna's face flush with pleasure, and she fanned her face with flapping fingers. "Whoo," she breathed.

"I know, right?" Toliq sat up and shimmied backward, pulling her skirt down to her knees. She looked from side to side through the corners of her sexy black-rimmed glasses, then began buttoning up her tight blouse. She finished the last button just below her neck, then began stuffing the bottom of the blouse into the waist of her skirt. "So, um, do you think Yahweh knows about the plot with our servant yet?"

"I'm hoping we threw him off track with that little circus at the board meeting," Inanna said. She rummaged in her purse and grabbed a pack of cigarettes. She flicked the softpack and four of the menthol 100's stood up. She pulled one out with her lips. Inanna rubbed the tip of her index finger and thumb together in a circular motion, massaging a few molecules of her own sweat until they combusted. She pinched the floating candle flame between her fingers and pushed the cigarette's tip gently into the fire. "He'll think our move has something to do with the board rather than with the humans. By the time Ghair Aadi's little bugs do their work, it will be too late."

Toliq beamed. "He's so lame. So lamestream, you know? Like, he thinks just whatever the thing would be that you might expect him to think. Golly." She shook her head. "Well, we'll just see where all that elite, booksmarts thinking gets him." She spit out the word "book" like it was made of acid.

Inanna took a deep drag on the cigarette, plastered on a genial smile, and said, "mmm-hmm."

"So, what do we do now?"

Inanna looked up the street at Basilica of Sacre Coeur. "We could go take a walk up there." She pointed at it with a nod.

"It's mine, you know. And when Yahweh goes down, I think I'll make some changes to it. Not architectural. It's pretty enough. But I remember when people behaved differently in temples. Back in Sumer, they'd drink themselves into stupors, inhale psychedelic incense, dance on their knees, whip their hair around in circles until they were too dizzy to stand, and then roll all over each other in an orgy that looked like a drunken ball of snakes. It was beautiful."

"And don't forget the sacrifices," Toliq said. She looked up at the sky, blinking perhaps at the glare through her glasses, or at memories, or because she was trying to imagine what Inanna had said.

"The Sumerians liked to burn the entrails of goats. Not very sexy."

"The Aztecs would cut the heads and feet off of turkeys and burn them for me before the priests ate the bird's meat. The meat made them sleepy, and I would give them dreams."

"What kind of dreams?" Inanna asked.

"Dreams of anger at the know-it-alls, with their calendars and surgeries and machines. Visions of grabbing those smug pasty-faced scientists by the hair, pulling their heads back," she grabbed the air with her fingers, clawing, and yanked back toward her shoulder, "and cutting their throats and then painting themselves in the blood to make themselves stronger."

Inanna sat up straighter. "And did they do it?"

"They were too afraid. I wasn't in charge. And I think more of a concern has been not within the priests, the mistakes that were made, not being able to react to the circumstances that those mistakes created in a real positive and professional and helpful way for the chief gods, dontcha know."

83

Inanna frowned a bit, but her face went placid almost instantly. She took another drag. "I understand," she lied. "But things will be different, soon." She popped up again. "Oh, you know what we should do?"

"What?"

"Human sacrifices!"

"Yeah!" Toliq nodded like a bobble-head doll. "Ooo, but who should we have them kill for us?"

"Well, at first it will be tribal. The Americans will blame the Muslims for Ghair Aadi's bugs, and they'll start bombing. We'll have the Muslims stoning Christians in no time." She hooked a thumb toward Sacre Coeur. "Pretty soon we'll have the French Catholics killing the Muslims here in Paris. All the while, they'll be getting sick and dying like flies. But eventually our hand-picked survivors will look for the new gods, and our prophets will start using our names. Who do you want them to kill for you, Honey?"

"Oh, I don't know. Teachers, I guess. And librarians. And lamestream journalists. Whoever refudiates us."

Inanna shrugged. "Yeah, that's good. But when they're gone, I think I'll have them kill post-menopausal women and impotent old men, then have orgies in their blood."

"I like that!" Toliq said.

Inanna stubbed out her cigarette on the roof, then looked up at Toliq with hungry eyes. "It makes you hot, doesn't it?"

Toliq's eyes went wide. "I guess it does!"

Inanna rocked up onto her knees, then slid her hands into Toliq's skirt, pushing her legs apart. "Wanna have another go?"

"You're darn right I do!"

11

"These directions can't be right," Christy said.

Joe made the turn off of OR-22 dictated by the single-page printout from Google maps. "Why not?"

Christy frowned at the page. "Well, Google has us going from 22, through three turns that all keep us on the same road, and we end up on 22 again."

"Let me see," Joe said, looking over.

"No, you just drive. We'll get there. I just wish you'd used MapQuest. Remember when we used Google Maps and they had us going the wrong way on a one way street?"

"That was like five years ago. It's gotten a lot more accurate. Plus, I think that was MapQuest."

Christy's face tightened into a dangerous scowl. "It was Google Maps. I remember."

It wasn't until she made that face that Joe realized she'd put on a bit more makeup than normal and was wearing a lower-cut dress than she had the last time they'd gone to one of these staff parties. When she'd come down the stairs to greet the babysitter, he'd commented on how nice she looked, but he hadn't really examined her too closely. Now he couldn't figure out quite what was different, beyond the cut of the dress. Was she really wearing more make-up? No, she'd just chosen a slightly darker shade of lipstick and had done something different with her eye shadow. He couldn't identify the fact that she'd used three colors in a more complex layering than normal because he wasn't an expert on such things. He admitted it looked good but felt hesitant about saying anything. Something about her make-up, and her scowl, made him anxious.

"Sorry," he mumbled.

"Oh, it's fine. Do you think these curves are the left, right, and left the directions say?"

They weren't. The road came to a T at a light, and they had to turn right to stay on the road. Then it curved off to the left while another road with a different name continued straight on. Another T and another right, and they came to 22 again.

"Oh, well, we were on 22 East, and now it's 22 North," Joe said.

Christy scowled again. "Yeah, I see that now, Joe."

He mouthed, "Sorry," but she didn't notice.

After two more turns (to stay on one more road) they found the house. Christy grumbled about the way Joe parked the car, then took her pesto salad out of the back seat and started up the hill toward the house, leaving him behind as he locked the doors. He caught her at the Bhatnagars' front door. A short, pretty woman in a yellow and orange sari opened it. She was wearing a sticker bindi on her forehead, the modern version of the traditional red dot popular in Southeast Asia. Hers had a silver half-moon on one side that matched her red and silver earrings. She smiled warmly and welcomed Joe and Christy into her home.

"Abhilasha, this is my husband, Joe. Joe, Abhilasha Bhatnagar."

"Nice to meet you," Joe said, realizing with some terror that there was absolutely no chance he'd remember the woman's name.

"Call me Abhi," the woman said.

Phew, Joe thought.

He followed the women into the kitchen as they discussed Christy's pesto salad. The house was a strange design. It was built on the hill overlooking West Salem. Its driveway led down to the garage under one side of the house, but the floors were all split level, so that a broad and decorative staircase led up from the foyer to the living room above the garage, and a separate thin, steep staircase led up to a smaller sitting room, followed by a study. Both the living room and the sitting room were already populated with professors and spouses. A large porch on the same level as the kitchen held a half-dozen people sitting at wooden tables or standing. Three people stood on the other porch, which extended beyond the living room and offered the best view of the city beyond the woods around the house. Everyone spoke in hushed tones, but the quantity of conversation created a warm buzz. In this low din, Joe almost missed Christy's voice.

She grabbed the sleeve of his shirt. "Joe?"

"Huh? Oh, sorry."

"Joe, this is Raktim, Abhilasha's husband."

Joe shook the man's hand. He had a thick, dark mustache and clever eyes. "You have a beautiful home," Joe said, and he wasn't just being polite. The walls of the kitchen were painted two different shades, one ochre, the other a rich orange. The walls of the sitting room up the stairs were white, and the walls of the living room were something darker than the kitchen, though the drawn shades made it difficult to make out what colors they were, exactly. Every wall held some piece of artwork, ranging from brightly colored tiled mosaics of the Virgin Mary from Mexico to a painting of Ganesh, his bright blue body and six arms visible from across the house, to smaller, wooden carvings from Africa and Japan.

"Oh, that's all Abhi's doing. She likes everyone to feel at home, so she has to have every color on the walls and art from all over the world."

"Well, it works. She has good taste," Joe said.

"I'm just glad she does all the painting herself. If she left it up to me, the walls would all still be white, and the only international flavor would be some furniture from Ikea."

Joe continued to look around, so Raktim filled the silence. "So, Joe, what do you do?"

"I sell insurance," Joe said.

"Oh, Joe, don't say it like that," Christy said. She turned to Raktim. "He runs the branch office for Prudential in Monmouth."

Joe shrugged. "I'm not sure middle management sounds much better than sales."

"Insurance, eh? I teach mathematics." Raktim said. "You could say you work in the practical application of large number theory."

"That does sound better. But I really don't do any math. The computer does all the calculating of the risk, the monthly rates, all that. What I do is really more like the practical application of the psychology of risk management."

"You try to get people to make logical decisions about the things they don't want to think about?" Raktim asked.

"Exactly."

"Then I know someone you should speak with," Raktim said. He put out an arm and, without actually touching Joe, guided him up the stairs out of the kitchen, toward the living room. Joe looked around and realized Christy and Abhi had disappeared.

Raktim led Joe into a conversation between an economics professor and a sociology professor. The subject turned to the nature of risk when he arrived, but eventually shifted to the attitudes of soldiers at war, and the incongruity of the American desire for bloodless wars and the soldier's need to ignore the risk of death in order to do her job effectively. Though Joe couldn't have imagined a conversation about war and peace evolving from a conversation about risk, now he'd never be able to think about war or peace without thinking of risk again. He didn't realize how much he was enjoying the conversation, and lost track of time.

"Joe, Mike," the sociology prof said, "I gotta hit the head. Want me to grab you guys another beer?"

Joe looked at his watch. "Thanks, Van, but I'd better check on Christy, see what time she wants to leave."

"Whipped," Van said as he left.

Joe shrugged. "Is he single?" he asked Mike.

"He and his wife have an understanding. He does whatever his wife says, and she lets him pretend he's the boss so he can look down on the rest of us."

Joe frowned and shook his head. "That sounds so great. I'm jealous." He rose to leave.

Mike called after him. "That's why he is better than us. Denial works, Joe. Trust me. I'm an economist."

Joe smiled and nodded as he wandered off through the mingling throng in the living room. He stepped into the sitting room and looked down the half-stairway into the kitchen. Scanning the people leaning on the bar or hovering around the food on the dinette table on the far side of the room, Joe didn't see Christy at first. Then he heard her laugh.

Partly obscured by the shoulders of a tall man in front of her, Christy was leaning against the stainless steel refrigerator door. As Joe stepped down the stairs, he got a better view of her. She held a drink in her left hand, though he couldn't see that through the man in front of her. He could see her right hand. As she recovered from the laugh, she bent her wrist and tilted the hand palm-up. She ever-so-slightly brushed the center of her sternum, just below her breasts, with the tip of her curved middle finger. No one else would have noticed, and really, there was nothing to notice, Joe thought. An itch, perhaps, caused by an uncomfortable bra. Or an absentminded search for a long necklace she wasn't wearing. Or nothing, just nothing at all.

The stairs were unusually steep and shallow. Joe's heel bobbled on the edge of one, then slid forward. He didn't lose his balance, just fell down one stair and landed heavily on the next. But in the split second of freefall he grabbed for the railing and looked down. By the time his hand had wrapped around the cold, black, wrought-iron railing, his foot was safely on the next step, but before he could look up at Christy an image flashed from his memory. Christy, leaning on their own refrigerator at home. She smiled at him, then dropped the smile like an actress practicing switching facial expressions as a warm-up before stepping onto the stage. With that overly serious face on, she raised her arm and bent her wrist slowly, then ran her middle finger up and down between her breasts once while winking at him. Then she over-articulated her words, Marilyn Monroe-style, "Hey, Big Boy. Wanna go upstairs and...fool around?" Then she'd bounced her eyebrows up and down, up and down, before she lost it and started laughing.

And they'd both laughed, laughed together good and hard before he grabbed her hand and they ran, clumping loudly, up the stairs. That was back before Dawkins was born, when they could clump up the stairs without fear of waking him. It was a different time.

The gesture, however, was the same. But so what? Joe thought. It didn't mean anything. And he wasn't the type to suspect that it did. He wasn't that type, he reminded himself.

He walked over to Christy but she didn't notice him until he was very close by. "Oh, hey!" she said, reaching out and wrapping that same right hand around the back of his arm just above the elbow. "Joe, this is Luke Devereaux, the new adjunct in my department."

Joe put out his hand, feeling Christy's slip off his elbow. Luke took it and shook it. Devereaux had a short, well-trimmed beard that didn't fit his hair, which was curly and unruly and a week away from crazy-homeless-guy hair. But behind his fashionable wire-rimmed glasses, Devereaux had genuine, guileless, kind eyes, and Joe couldn't help but like him immediately.

"It's nice to meet you, Luke," Joe said. "Christy has been talking about how they needed to bring somebody else in to get those class sizes down. She speaks very highly of you."

"Well, thanks," Luke said. "Everybody's been very welcoming."

"So, always a Luke and never a Lucas, right?"

"Did she tell you that?"

"No, just my guess," Joe said.

"That's right. And thanks for asking. Some people just assume they can launch right into Lucas, which isn't even my given name. And, believe it or not, sometimes 'Lucky.'"

"Let me guess: Salesmen," Joe said.

"Usually yes, but one was a cop who'd pulled me over. Speeding. Outside of Des Moines, Iowa."

"Did you get the ticket?" Joe said.

"Nope."

"Lucky didn't, but Luke would have," Joe said.

"Exactly!"

Christy smiled at Joe, then told Luke, "Joe runs an insurance agency, but he used to be a salesman, so he's really good at guessing people."

"Ah," Luke said, "so you could probably teach psychology better than the psych Ph.D.s in here."

Joe shook his head. "No, no. Those who can't teach have to do. I could never be a good professor like Christy. And when I see what she has to do, and what she has to put up with…well, frankly I'd rather go back to the days of cold calling my way through a phone book."

Christy held a hand up to her face and fake-whispered, "They used to actually do that!"

"Yes, I am old," Joe said. "I've been around since before micro-targeting and Internet data mining, since the days of phone books. I'm a dinosaur."

"Don't feel bad. When I started teaching, I had a chalkboard. Complete with chalk."

"No, really?" Christy asked, genuinely surprised. "Where was that?"

Luke regaled them both with stories from his undergrad at Tulane and his Ph.D. at the University of Iowa. (Which, Joe learned, is in Iowa City, not Des Moines. Drake is in Des Moines, and Luke got his ticket while driving back from visiting his girlfriend there. An ex-girlfriend.) Christy competed with her stories of long drives from her Ph.D. program at University of Oregon, in Eugene, to visit her boyfriend, an entry-level insurance salesman and recent graduate of Western University in Monmouth. Joe thought about making some crack about how the girlfriend from Drake was nowhere to be found while the boyfriend from Western was standing right next to the two Ph.D.s in the kitchen, but he couldn't figure out a funny punch line, let alone one that wouldn't put Luke on the spot. He clearly hadn't known the guy long enough to be teasing him about being an old bachelor, so Joe quietly let the two launch into stories about their Ph.D. courses.

"So, you came here from Iowa?" he asked Luke.

"No," Christy said. Then she caught herself and looked at the linoleum.

Luke squashed the awkwardness quickly. "I spent the last few years in New York, working as an adjunct at NYU. But it wasn't tenure track, so Western is a step up."

"Did you like New York?" Joe asked.

"Loved it. Have you ever been?"

"No. My dad lived there as a kid, but he never had a good thing to say about it. But my father's opinions don't hold a lot of weight with me, so...."

"Yeah, you really need to visit some time. I think lots of people have the wrong idea about the city from TV shows. It's a great place."

"So, how are you adjusting to small-town living?"

Luke smiled and nodded. "It's an adjustment, I admit, but there are some things I prefer about it."

Joe wanted to ask for specifics, but didn't want to put Luke on the spot.

Christy hoped she was on the list, but couldn't decide how she'd like to be described there.

So they talked about a national news story about a kidnapped little girl from a state none of them had ever visited, because that was more comfortable.

When Abhilasha came in with some plates she'd cleared from the porch, Joe found himself washing them. When Abhi returned a second time he found himself being scolded. Eventually Joe reminded Christy that the babysitter was still on the clock, and they left.

As they drove through the darkness, winding their way along the curves toward the highway that would take them back to Independence, Joe said, "Luke seems like a nice guy."

"Yeah," Christy said, "I guess."

Joe couldn't help it. It was dangerous to look away from the road, even for a split second, but he risked it.

Christy's hand rose from her lap, twisted up, and she rubbed the spot at the bottom of her bra again.

But it was nothing.

12

Two angels, their faces so blank they might as well not have had features at all, walked out of the kitchen, one after the other, and paced their steps so that they could set the steaming plates down in front of Yahweh and Frigga at exactly the same time.

"Thank you, Simha," Yahweh said to the angel who'd delivered His meal, but she'd already turned her back and didn't slow as she walked back into the kitchen.

The table wasn't one of those ridiculous, stretched-out affairs used in movies to show that rich characters are garish and distant, but it was a bit too long for God's liking. Eight feet felt like 10 when Frigga was at the other end.

"Did I ever mention the irony of Simha's name?" He asked.

Frigga put a forkful of meat into her mouth, looked up at Him, but did not speak.

"It means 'joyful' in Hebrew. But she never smiles. Ever."

"She is joyful because she serves you," Frigga said. "You know that smiling is just an outward sign of joy, and generally of the simplest kind. Also, she is trying to be as professional as possible. I think she's excellent."

"She is."

"You are angry at me for not speaking to you enough," Frigga said. With her Norse accent, Yahweh sometimes found it difficult to tell when she was making a statement and when she was asking a question. Or maybe that was because she so rarely asked questions.

"Trying not to be."

"You knew I would come to Simha's defense," she said.

"Mm-hmm."

"We've had this exact conversation before."

"Really?" God asked.

Frigga took a bite, so it was her turn to respond with her lips closed. "Mm-hmm."

"Did it work last time, too?"

That got a smile, if only a small one. "Yahweh-leh, tell me what you want to talk about."

God liked it when His wife used his Hebrew pet name. He used her Norse one in turn. "Min-Frigga-Kjære, things at work are…I don't know…rough lately."

"Explain."

"Inanna is making a move of some kind. I can't figure it out. It's been weighing on me."

Frigga shook her head. "You know I never liked that girl. But step-mothers have to be extra careful. It's too easy to be the evil step-mother. Better to not say anything."

"You said so."

"To you. Not to Jesus. Maybe I should have." Frigga found it impossible to speculate about what might have been if different decisions were made. Because she knew the future perfectly, she couldn't conceive of a different past which might have led up to a different present. Consequently, whenever she thought of the past, she got frustrated. Yahweh tried to keep her from thinking about the past as much as He could.

He speculated for her as He chewed His next bite. "Wouldn't have made any difference. He doesn't like authority figures much."

"He loves you," Frigga said. She looked up at Him, hard.

"He loves everybody. That doesn't mean he likes them."

She bent her head forward and looked at him through her eyebrows. "He likes you, too."

"You think so?"

Frigga nodded slowly. That was her way of saying she knew something for sure.

They ate in silence for a moment.

"So, do you know what Inanna is planning?" Yahweh asked.

She took another bite. "Mm-hmm." She smiled again.

"What is it?"

"Nothing that changes my opinion."

"Of her?"

"Not that, either," Frigga said.

"What do you mean?"

"Nothing that changes my opinion of her, but, more importantly, nothing that changes my opinion of you. Of what you should do."

"Is it going to be bad?" God asked.

"It doesn't have to be bad for you."

"Because I could retire." Yahweh shook His head. "You know I don't want to retire."

"I know."

More silence. God thought about how to phrase His question.

"Does Inanna's plan incline you to want me to retire more than you would otherwise?"

"There is no otherwise for me. You know that."

God felt the way He always did when He talked with His wife about the future: Frustrated. Of course, they both knew the future, but they knew it in different ways. He couldn't understand the way she knew it. It was not His way. It seemed so fatalistic.

"If she were to force you to retire, you would be retired. If you choose to retire, you would be retired."

"And what? Playing bocce ball and shuffleboard with Zeus and Hadad and Osiris? You saw him at lunch yesterday. You want me to be like that?"

"You won't be like that."

"True, but you know that someday, when I am playing bocce ball and shuffleboard, it will make a difference to me, how I went out."

"Some days it will, and some days it won't," Frigga said.

Yahweh thought about saying, "You know, Frigga, you being just this damned helpful is the reason your ex-husband, Odin, is playing bocce ball with those other geezers." But He knew that would wound her, and what was the point of that? He'd just feel guilty later.

"Just think about it some more," Frigga said.

"I will."

They ate in silence for a moment.

Yahweh frowned and looked up at His wife. "Why do you try to persuade me, anyway? You know what I will choose."

"I don't try," she said. "I persuade you because that's what I've always known I must do, and you decide when I've always known you would decide, and we will always come to the same place because we do. Maybe you would have decided at a different time if I hadn't tried to persuade you. I don't know that."

Yahweh could tell she was getting frustrated with herself again. He was getting frustrated too, but not with her. Despite her cryptic reply, He understood, at least somewhat. For Frigga, even her actions were known in advance. He'd asked her more than once if she felt that she had free will, or if that was stolen from her by her knowledge of the future. For her, this question was unanswerable, like speculating about the sound of a tree falling in a forest if no one, not even Yahweh Himself, heard it. She could barely understand "will," let alone "free." She did what she knew she would do. And so did everyone else.

"Min-Frigga-Kjære?" He asked as gently as He could.

"Yes, Yahweh-leh?"

"Will I retire before Inanna's plan takes effect?"

Frigga looked down at her plate, closed her eyes slowly, opened them and pushed the plate forward, then looked up at her husband. "Her plan has already begun to have effects, Yahweh-leh." She pushed her lips together tightly and swallowed hard. She closed her eyes again. Frigga was not one to cry, but when she opened her eyes, they were wet. "It has already begun."

13

They met him in the parking lot. Baldur grabbed him and hugged him so hard he lifted him off the ground. When he set him down, Baldur kept one arm around his shoulders, and it was a good thing, because Baldur's half-brother, Thor, slapped Jesus so hard on the back he would have knocked him onto his face on the smooth, gold pavement. Thor was so strong, Jesus suspected he was wasting half his eternal life in the gym.

"Jesus Christ! It is so good to see you out of your house, my friend!" Thor cried.

Baldur squeezed him around the shoulders. "Hear, hear!"

Jesus smiled, but said, "Careful, guys. You're going to crush me. Remember, I'm all God and all Man."

"Oh, yeah, I'd forgotten that," Thor admitted.

"I hadn't, but it never made any sense to me in the first place," Baldur said.

"I don't fully understand it, either," Jesus admitted.

Baldur released Jesus, then pushed playfully at his shoulder. "So, who else is coming tonight?"

"Apollo, Hephaestus, Artemis—"

"A woman?" Thor shouted. "I left Sif at home. I thought this was a guy's night out."

Baldur laughed. "Artemis is more man than you, Thor. Besides, try and separate her from Apollo, and they'd probably both kick your ass."

"That's what I figured," Jesus said. "I invited Muhammad, but you know he'd never set foot in this kind of place." He looked up at the giant neon sign above them. It blinked blue, then purple, then red. White lights blinked on and off around the words in sequence, creating the impression that the light moved around in a clockwise motion. Inside that turning circle, in a fancy, swooping font, the club's name glowed: "Bacchanalia."

"I also invited Sobek and Khepri," Jesus continued.

Baldur shot Thor a look, and Thor shrugged.

"What?" Jesus asked.

"Nothing. Those guys creep me out, that's all. But it's cool."

"I just thought, you know, I haven't seen them in a long time, either," Jesus said.

"Oh, yeah, no, it's fine," Baldur said. "You're right. They should be here. Verily, it's my hang-up. They just weird me out a little."

"I think you'll like them better when you get to know them."

Thor chuckled, and even that made a booming sound when Thor did it. "Of course you think that. Forsooth, you love everybody."

"But I don't like everybody. These guys I like."

Baldur slapped Jesus on the back, not as hard as Thor had, but still hard. "Then that's good enough for me," he said, but Jesus wondered if the heavy slap on the back was a way of saying the opposite.

They waited in silence for a moment. Jesus noted, appreciatively, that Baldur and Thor had chosen to dress down for the occasion. Baldur, Norse god of light, beauty, happiness, and love, wore blue jeans and a simple black t-shirt, and hadn't bothered to change his regular unearthly white skin and bright blond hair. His beard hung a bit longer than Thor's, but not as long as Jesus' dark curly one. It glowed faintly, like the hair on his head.

Thor's skin wasn't the symbolic white of Baldur's, but he still chose a fair Norwegian's flesh and straight blond locks. His hair was only slightly wavier than Baldur's and hung to his shoulders, while his beard was neatly trimmed and a bit darker than his golden curls. His shirt was black, like Baldur's, but advertised for the band Metallica. His pants were made of shiny black leather, and his giant hammer hung from his belt as always, tiny tendrils of lightening dancing across its shiny surface every once in a while. While Baldur stood only a couple inches taller than Jesus, Thor towered over them both. He'd once been the Norse god of lightning, thunder, strength, fertility, courage, and the protection of mankind. It had been a big job, requiring a big god. Now his patronage was diminished. He was the god of professional wrestling, American football, and other forms of combat-as-entertainment. His chosen physical form spoke of a longing for his lost larger role.

For some reason, part of the all God and all Man mantle meant that Jesus couldn't change his shape like the other immortals. He still looked like a swarthy Semitic guy of slightly above-average height, just as he had for the last couple millennia. Above average height in Roman-occupied Palestine was not as tall as your average cab driver in Helsinki, and gods tended toward the tall side, so Jesus felt tiny next to Baldur and figured he could take a nap in Thor's shade. Jesus hadn't trimmed his beard since his meeting with Muhammad, and it had grown into large ringlets that hung over his Adam's apple. His hair probably would have been longer than Thor's if it were straight, but it began to curl above his ears and hinted at the Jew-fro it could become by the time it reached his jawline. He'd put on some clean khakis he'd found in a heap in the bottom of his closet and an olive green t-shirt with a red image of Che Guevara on the front. Unlike his Norse friends, who both wore heavy boots, he'd pulled on a pair of well-worn Chuck Taylors. As they stood in silence, he looked down at his feet and noticed his wrinkled pants. The lips of the side pockets were bent and curling up. Still, compared to the sweatpants he'd been wearing for the last few hundred years, he felt downright presentable.

The three looked up as Artemis and Hephaestus arrived. The Greeks floated in gracefully, but when they landed, Hephaestus allowed himself to limp in a rhythmic pimp-walk that made one of his massive, rounded shoulders spin in a little orbit. He'd worn his usual red hair as curly as Jesus' and as long as Thor's, though his posture made his long, wide beard hang onto his broad chest. His wife-beater undershirt was mostly hidden by his denim overalls.

Artemis wore a chin almost as pointy as the heels of her thigh-high leather boots. Her shirt clasped on the side with a gold brooch, and though it was tight around her small chest, the bright purple fabric hung more loosely near her waist, hinting at a toga she might have worn to a more formal occasion. She had the kind of beauty that made men ogle her while smashing their cars into telephone poles; her legs and arms were long and strong, and her walk was as aggressive as her eyes.

Hephaestus lunged toward Jesus and his hand shot out, clasping Jesus' in a smothering grip. Then he pulled Jesus close and hugged him with his other arm. When released, Jesus looked at his friend's beaming smile. "Look at you!" Hephaestus said. "Out of the basement! I am so glad to see you."

"It's good to see you, too." Jesus reached out and offered his free hand to Artemis, who shook it. "And Artemis, how are you?"

The goddess looked up at the neon lights of Bacchanalia, then back to Jesus. "Hunting, as always," she said, and winked at him.

"Where's your brother?"

She rolled her eyes. "He always prefers to drive."

They looked across the parking lot at the approaching cars, but Jesus' Egyptian friends had beaten Apollo to the club. Pulling their shiny black jeep into a spot nearby, Khepri and Sobek climbed out. Sobek, the driver, pushed his door closed, then looked over at Jesus and grinned broadly. Of course, he always grinned broadly, because he had the head of a crocodile, but Jesus was pretty sure he'd earned a bigger smile than usual. Khepri's features made his emotions inscrutable; though his body was a man's, he had the complete body of a dung beetle for a head. When he reached Jesus, his raspy, deep voice vibrated through the round abdomen that made up the lower part of his face. "Jezzuz, I waz zo glad you called. I havvve been vvvery conzzzerned about you."

"I'm sorry I worried you, Khepri. I'm doing better. In fact, I'm feeling really good tonight."

Jesus shook hands with Khepri, then with Sobek. Sobek blinked his crocodile eyes slowly. "I have missed you greatly."

"I'm sorry I haven't called. It's good to see you."

The Norse and Greek gods shook hands with the Egyptians. Baldur smiled pleasantly and hid his discomfort with Jesus' Egyptian friends' appearances. Then all seven of them turned and looked across the parking lot, alerted by the loud roar of the oncoming car. Artemis made a disgusted little choking sound.

The car had the body of a Lamborghini Murciélago LP640 Roadster, only instead of the usual black, red, yellow, or green paintjobs, the car itself glowed so brightly the gods in the parking lot had to shield their eyes from the yellow-white light. Through his fingers, Jesus noticed the license plate. It was blue with yellow writing, like a plate from California, though California was an infinite distance from The City. The vanity plate said, "Helios."

The car screamed into a space near the Egyptian's jeep, and the driver's side door raised up in that characteristic Lamborghini way. The figure who stepped out was just a silhouette while the door slid back down into place, but he turned and clicked a button on his keychain. There was a loud beep, and the car's sun-bright glow fell in on itself, leaving a cinder black car that didn't even reflect the light of all the neon around them.

"Jesus!" Apollo cried, throwing his arms wide. He looked like Robert Redford, but glowing instead of leathery. Not spackled in glitter like a teenage girl's vampire dream, and not blinding like Helios' car had been, but glowing like the Truth with a capital T.

Jesus stepped forward and gave his friend a hug, but couldn't tear his eyes off the car. "Hey," he mumbled.

Apollo followed Jesus' eyes. "Quite a chariot, eh? Helios let me borrow it. It's a hell of a lot of car. I can see why he won't let his son drive it."

Khepri made a clicking sound. Jesus wondered if it was an expression of appreciation or jealousy. "Great car," Khepri told Apollo.

"I knew you'd be able to appreciate it," Apollo said to the Egyptian god of the dawn. "Artemis hates when I borrow it. She thinks it's tacky."

"I do," she said. "It's garish! Don't you all think so?"

Sobek looked at her and nodded. "I'm with you," he said. "I've seen Pyramids that were less desperate looking."

"Exactly!" Artemis said, motioning toward the car with an upturned hand while looking at Sobek. "It's too much."

Hephaestus tried to defend the car on the grounds of its engineering, but Baldur and Thor scoffed at Italian design.

"Too cute," Baldur said.

"Overrated," Thor said.

"Well, if you guys don't mind, I'll leave you boys to your toys while I go in and try to get my pick of the women before you get inside," Artemis said.

"No chance," Apollo said, pushing her aside playfully and leading the whole group toward the club.

When they reached the entrance, the bouncer, a large, scaled angel who looked a bit like Yahweh's bodyguard Uriel, complete with the dangerously clawed fingers and 16 reptilian wings, waved them through with a tired gesture. The troop made their way through a short, dark hall, and the sound of the pulsing music grew with each step, until they stepped into the club itself and the music exploded around them, shaking smiles onto their faces and vibrating Jesus' sternum with each beat of the heavy bass.

Bacchanalia was the hippest club in all of the City. Part discothèque, part strip club, and all bar, the single massive main room contained levels made by sunken floors and elevated stages. A huge ring of a bar wrapped around the main stage in the middle of the room, and another wrapped around the room's edge, but the latter was broken up by doorways leading to private rooms and, on the far side, a number of tables set into alcoves in the back wall. Rings of dancing neon also wrapped around the room, beginning fifteen feet above the floor and set within one another at slightly odd angles. When the lights flickered on and off, it could create the impression that red, blue, and purple light climbed up five stories toward the room's ceiling. Or, if the song called for it, the light could be made to climb down the walls. At irregular intervals, the lights could even blink in such a way as to create the illusion that the neon energy swirled around the room, sometimes clockwise, sometimes counterclockwise. This could make a dancer that much dizzier. Simply being in the room made a person feel pleasantly drunk, and with addition of alcohol it could make patrons fall onto one another in tangles of flailing arms and legs and still-gyrating hips. Jesus looked up at the dancers spinning around poles on the various stages throughout the room, currently two on the main stage and eight others on the stages scattered throughout. Some of the stages stood just a few feet above the higher levels of the floor, while others were made of glass and poked out of the walls 20 and 30 feet above the roiling crowd. How did those dancers spin around like that in a room where the walls themselves seemed to rise, fall, and turn, without stumbling sideways and falling off their stages onto the customers? he wondered. Lots of practice, he guessed.

The group stepped up to the bar below the main stage.

"Is Bacchus in?" Apollo asked the bartender, a man with a thick handlebar mustache and eyebrows that said his mood was just pleasant enough for customer service.

"I think he's up in his office. Want me to call him for you?"

"No, that's okay. I'll take a glass of the best wine you've got."

"A Nectar for me," Artemis said, though she was staring up at the nearest dancer.

"Two flagons of mead for my brother and me," Baldur said.

"And two pitchers to keep those full," Thor shouted.

"That zzzzoundzzz good," Khepri said to Thor. "I'll have a flagon of that mead, too."

Thor laid a heavy hand on the Egyptian god's shoulder and beamed. "Good choice!" Then he took a slight step backward, unsure how far he'd have to move to get out of the line of sight of a god with no eyes, and made a funny face at his brother, removing his hand slowly from its place inches from a dung beetle.

Sobek asked for a Nectar with a straw. He had a hard time drinking from a glass, and a drooling crocodile can be off-putting.

Hephaestus ordered a Scotch for himself and one for Jesus. Jesus accepted, though he would have preferred Apollo's wine.

They began looking for a table, Apollo pulling Artemis along because she was transfixed by one of the strippers on the main stage. They circumnavigated the crowded dance floor and made their way to a table set in an alcove in the back of the club. A waiter, an angel with feathered wings like Gabriel's, came to take their order, folding back the seven pairs of wings that wrapped around his whole body and revealing a slight torso and two long, thin hands holding a notepad and a pencil so short it looked more appropriate for keeping score in a game of miniature golf. The Norse gods ordered another pitcher of mead, though they hadn't started drinking yet, because they wanted to be stocked.

Jesus sat at the C-shaped table's outside edge, his shoulders turned in toward his party, so when the fingers gently tapped on his shoulder, he was taken by surprise.

"Oh my gawd, it is you!" the woman said. She wore a pair of thong underwear, a wide leather belt with some kind of white fur on it, and matching knee high leather boots with white fur around the knees. She also had earrings on. They looked like dreamcatchers. Other than that, she was as naked as her profession demanded.

"Hello," Jesus said. It wasn't quite a question, but he was cautious.

"Wow, oh my gawd, okay, okay," the woman's voice fell as she tried to collect herself. She took a deep breath, made all the more dramatic by her toplessness, then fell down on her knees, her hands on Jesus' leg, one on his knee and the other too high for comfort. "Okay, Jesus, I have been waiting to meet you so I can say thank you." She was looking down at the ground, which made Jesus just a bit more uncomfortable. "I have been hoping you'd come in here for like, I don't know, like 30 years, because I wanted to thank you so much, so much..." she leaned back, sitting on her feet, "for the new body you have given me!" She threw back her shoulders and flipped her long, straight, dark brown hair so that it trailed down her spine toward her only clothing. She looked like something that might have been found in an early seventies Playboy riding the wave of the era's Native American chic, and Jesus suspected that might have been exactly where her definition of the perfect body had come from. "I just love it," she continued, "and it's all thanks to you."

"Well, I can't take all the credit," Jesus tried.

"No, see, I used to be fat and ugly and my pretty friends kept me around just to feel better about themselves and I felt awful all the time," the stripper said.

Jesus put a hand over hers, the one on his knee. "But Sarah Elizabeth, I loved you then," Jesus said.

"Well, sure you did, but a hell of a lot of good that did me back then, right?" She laughed at the self-evident nature of her own statement. "But I had this youth pastor who told me that when I got here I would get a new body, a perfect body, and that gave me hope."

"Well, I'm glad your pastor was so good to you," Jesus said.

"Oh, no, he was horrible. He'd do these private counseling sessions with the girls where he'd try to make us feel bad about the way we looked, then counsel the fatties or the bulemics or the anorexics just so he could do stuff to us. And he was married. He never like, cheated-cheated on his wife, but he'd grope us girls and make out with the slutty ones. He was terrible!"

"That's—"

"I know, right? But somehow I knew that what he said about new bodies was true, and I wanted that so bad, and I prayed for it. Then, I died just because that bitch Lorna McDonald couldn't handle her liquor and swore she was fine to drive and ran her Ford Grenada off the side of the road into a tree and my fat ass went through the windshield and I died. I died. She lived and cried a little for her fat friend and then went on to get married to the perfect guy and have a couple beautiful kids. No fair, right?"

Jesus tried to say something.

"But now I'm here and I changed my name to Cherokie and I'm working here and happier than I've ever been, and I hear she has stretchmarks and big flab under her arms that waves when she does, and one of her teenagers is making her miserable, and of course I don't want her to be unhappy but it's just like, just desserts, right?"

Thor raised his glass. "A toast to Schadenfreude!" he cried, and everyone at the table but Jesus drank.

Jesus patted the stripper's hand. "Well, Sarah Elizabeth, um, Cherokie, I'm glad you're happy."

"Yeah, so I just wanted to say blessed is the womb that bore you and the breasts that nursed you!" As she said this she took her hands from his leg, but his relief was fleeting because she decided a measure of deaf signs was necessary, first squeezing her crotch, then cupping both breasts. "So, like, can I give you a free lapdance to say thank you? Or whatever you want. Really," she said, and winked in such an exaggerated way Jesus thought she might pull a muscle in her face, "I do mean whatever you want."

"Um, that's okay," Jesus said. He tried to remember his line. "Uh, blessed rather are those who hear the word of God and obey it."

"Oh, okay," Cherokie said, and Jesus could see a bit of sadness flicker in her large, unnaturally blue eyes. Those used to be brown, Jesus remembered. He'd liked those better.

"Weak!" Hephaestus barked. "Jesus, you're going to hurt the poor girl's feelings. Cherokie, I'll take one of those lap dances. That new body you've picked out for yourself is positively smelting."

"And I'm next," Artemis said. "I like your style." The goddess pointed at the stripper, then aimed her finger up and down slowly, lingering on her favorite parts. "And if that 'whatever' offer is still open…." Artemis mimicked Cherokie's exaggerated wink, and everyone laughed.

Jesus stood so Hephaestus could slide out, but instead Cherokie slipped past and climbed into the booth. The former Sarah Elizabeth straddled the lame god, sank her fingers into his beard, and used it as handles to pull herself backward and forward as she rode him. This particularly pleased the other bearded gods. Then she started brushing her nipples against Hephaestus' mustache and the tip of his nose while she swung her hair in wide helicopter circles. Most of the gods appreciated this, too, but the third time her heavy tresses smacked Jesus in the back of his head he quietly slipped out of the booth, grabbed a chair from a nearby table, and switched to the other side so that he now sat by Baldur and could watch the show from a safe distance.

Baldur leaned sideways. "You don't like her?"

"No, it's not that. I just feel bad for her, and…" His voice trailed off, and he picked up his glass of Scotch. He took a hefty swig until the ice cubes fell against his mustache. The Scotch was smooth at first, but burned like boiling acid just between his lungs. Then he looked back at Baldur, only to find his friend still staring at him, an eyebrow cocked and waiting.

Baldur said nothing.

"And I'm still married," Jesus said.

Baldur smiled. "'Still?'"

"Yeah."

"As in 'still for now but not forever'?"

Now it was Jesus' turn to smile a bit. "I guess so."

Baldur reeled back, bouncing against the cushion of the booth, and slapped Jesus on the back. "It's about sodding time!"

Everyone at the table looked over at this. Everyone except Hephaestus and Artemis, who were now sharing Cherokie who straddled a leg of each and alternately ran her fingers through their hair, then gripped handfuls and pulled their heads in toward her breasts as she writhed on them.

Baldur looked quickly at Jesus. "Are you keeping it a secret?"

"Well, I need to keep it a secret from Inanna," he said.

Both Sobek and Keprhi hissed when they heard Inanna's name. Sobek's hiss was low and slow. Khepri's was a quick intake followed by a series of rapid clicks that sounded a bit like high-pitched, rapid repetitions of the word "Cunt."

"None of us are big fans or your wife, Jesus," Apollo said.

Artemis put a hand on Cherokie's shoulder, shoving the woman chest-first into Hephestus' face as she leaned around her. "We talking about Inanna?" She pointed an accusative finger at Jesus. "I've told you before, she's a twat and I will never like her. I'm sorry, but I'm just saying."

Jesus threw up his hands in a gesture of concession.

"Okay, that's all I'm saying," she said, and disappeared into Cherokie's bosom again.

Thor elbowed Baldur. "So what's the big secret?"

Baldur looked at Jesus, who took a deep breath, swallowed, and said, "I'm going to divorce Inanna."

Thor grabbed his glass so fast it splashed mead onto the table, where it bounced up onto Cherokie's back. "Hey!" she cried, spinning a bit too fast and driving her knee into Hephaestus' crotch. While the stripper apologized to an angry god, the others congratulated Jesus.

"It izzzz about damned time," Kehpri said.

Sobek just threw the top of his crocodile head back like he was yawning, then let out a great whoop of exultation.

Only Apollo frowned and leaned across the table toward Jesus as the other drank. "You will have to be very careful with this, Jesus. She's dangerous."

"Oh, I know," Jesus said, and laughed. "Boy, do I know it!"

Apollo shook his head. "No, my young friend, you do not. It may be that Inanna has not changed much since you two last spoke, but the circumstances have changed. Her power has grown. She has new allies, dangerous ones you need to take seriously."

Jesus nodded, suddenly sober. "I know of some of them."

"Well, I think we have some planning to do," Baldur said. "Step one, Jesus, you send Cherokie over to my half-brother while Apollo and I explain the situation to Hephaestus and Artemis. Then, once Cherokie has departed, we can move on to step two."

117

Jesus stood and moved to the other side of the table, where he directed Cherokie to the Norse gentlemen with a tap on the shoulder and a gesture in their direction. Then he pulled his chair over to Hephaestus' side of the table while Cherokie climbed onto Thor's lap and went to work. Artemis leaned against Hephaestus, and Apollo rested his head on his twin's shoulder so he could hear about Jesus' situation again.

When Artemis heard Jesus' decision, she reached out and grabbed his shoulder, giving it a hard squeeze, and made an undignified squeal.

Once Cherokie was finished with her... dance? demonstration? advertisement which is, in itself, the product? she accepted the thanks of the gods at the table, along with tips, which were passed discretely but worn like state fair ribbons on the hip of the dancer's thong. Jesus made an attempt, feeble as it was, to convince Cherokie that he was pleased by her happiness. She grabbed his head and pulled him into a sort of hug where her breast was pressed against the side of his face. "You're so sweet," she said, and left.

"We may have to take care of her. She heard about your plan, Jesus," Apollo said.

Artemis watched Cherokie swish away. "I think I can hold onto her until it's safe to let her go," she offered.

"Good," Apollo said seriously.

Jesus looked at Artemis. "But you won't hurt her, right?"

Artemis thought about making some quip, then smiled at Jesus gently. "No. Don't worry."

He turned back to Apollo. "Do you really think Inanna would find out from Sarah Elizabeth?"

Sobek lay a human-shaped hand over Apollo's, then opened his crocodile mouth. "Jesus, your wife likes to kill girls for fun.

Her greatest joy is a drug-fueled orgy ending in the ritual sacrifice of a virgin."

Jesus looked at Cherokie across the bar. "I'm sure she's safe from that particular ceremony, but I see your point. But there used to be lots of ritual sacrificing. You guys had all kinds of goats and cows slaughtered in your names. That kind of thing is past, right? My Church doesn't do that."

Kheprhi shook his head. "Your houzzzez of worjjjip form a great zzzzzzkkkitzzzzophrenikkk inzzzztitujjjjion now, Jezzuz."

Baldur nodded. "They preach your love and Inanna's hatred. They obsess about sex but deny thine followers even a good wank, turning that frustration into a power they can direct. Then Inanna wields them like my half-brother's hammer or the good huntress' bow. Her schemes are so complex they boggle the mind. It will seem that she serves Ekekko, and your church will bring greater power to the wealthy. But then it might seem this serves Horus, when the church strengthens the hands of those already steeped in power. And always Enlil is in her ear, whispering his magic spells of talking points so that she will have them spoken from your pulpits. Lately, she has been accompanied by Chalchiuhtotoliq, perhaps as a kind of apprentice or perhaps as a lover." Baldur looked down at the table. "Your wife, as you know, is not faithful to you."

Jesus nodded. "This Chalchiuhtotoliq? What is her domain?"

Hephaestus leaned forward. "She goes by Toliq. She was an Aztec mystery goddess. Night turkeys, if I remember correctly. She disappeared from the scene for a while, but reappeared, introduced at a grand party thrown by her cousin Ayauhteotl. Ayauhteotl has reinvented herself quite successfully, too. She was the Aztec goddess of mist, fog, vanity, and fame. Now she's the American goddess of unfounded celebrity. She has many worshippers. But her priests, these reality TV stars and spoiled heiresses, they have no particular ambition to anything beyond feeding their own vanity with more fame. Annoying, but pretty harmless. It seems this Toliq has staked out a territory as the goddess of American anti-intellectualism, and she has designs on dominion over the Earth."

"Why? What would that even look like?" Jesus asked him. "I don't get it."

"Of course you don't," Apollo said. "You want a world filled with love and peace. A place where people care for one another and see that as the highest good. She wants a world where they hate learning itself, where language devolves slowly, where logic breaks into pieces buried under the weight of indescribable intuitions."

"But that's terrible!"

Apollo shook his head. "No, it's just a choice. Remember, Jesus, your world of peace and love isn't the one we would all have. Not a lot of noble combat for Thor there."

Jesus looked to Thor. "But surely you'd prefer my world to one filled with drooling idiots stumbling into one another, right?"

Thor shrugged. "There is little honor among fools, but, though it would take great courage to make a world without war, it would be a hollow victory to me, because how would future courage be recognized?" Then the big god smiled. "Worry not, my friend. Methinks Inanna has amassed forces so great, your Heaven on Earth is far from becoming my Hell on Earth. Should we come to that bridge, we might find ourselves at odds, but for now I stand with you, as I think there will be many an empty skull to crush with my hammer in the army you will face if you oppose your whore of a wife."

Jesus found Thor's loyalty oddly comforting, probably due to his friend's straightforwardness and predictability.

"Thor," he said, "it is always good to have friends who are true to themselves. I am glad you are and remain Thor."

"And it is good to have friends who demand as much. You make me your friend by wanting me to be Thor."

Apollo's smile fell. "Um, guys, I'm a Greek god, so I love a good homoerotic discussion about the nature of friendship as much as the next bisexual god, but I think we have a problem."

He nodded to the figures who'd just stepped out of the hallway and were circling the main stage, heading in their direction.

Sobek turned his big crocodile head toward Apollo and tried to whisper, "Shouldn't someone grab the Galilean before—"

It was too late. Jesus was already out of Hephaestus' reach, though the lame god grabbed for him as he went.

Artemis looked to Baldur. "Will you be able to control your half-brother?"

Lightening flashed in Thor's wide, excited blue eyes. "Fight!" he barked, and he leapt after Jesus.

Baldur looked at Artemis, shook his head, and shrugged.

14

Luke Devereaux unlocked the door to his two bedroom apartment and stepped inside, hugging a full paper bag stuffed with his week's groceries. Next to the door, at eye level, hung a mirror with a shelf above some small hooks. Luke hung his keys on the first hook on the left, then caught a glimpse of himself in the mirror as he turned. It created a curious illusion; instead of seeing himself, he saw the apartment as he walked to the kitchen with the groceries, the sparse decorations and his own framed head among them.

The furniture was a rough collection of Ikea, Fred Meyer's, and Target purchases made on an ad hoc basis as he realized what he needed. He'd come from New York with only two bags, with a few trunks of knick-knacks and hard copies of files mailed along afterward. He hadn't even had a car when he arrived. Hadn't needed one in New York. And his furniture hadn't been worth shipping. Not even his TV. Barely worth the trouble of the Craig's List ads.

But the apartment wasn't empty. He'd bought a blocky, dark brown coffee table which didn't quite match the black entertainment center that held his new TV, a modest 32-inch flat screen. The coffee table did match the end tables on either side of the white denim-covered Ikea couch, because he'd bought the end tables at Target with the coffee table. The Target tables held twin Ikea reading lamps with white shades covered with an appliqué like the skirts of tiny wedding dresses. There, among that furniture, Luke saw his own face. Almost tasteful. Yes, that was true of both, but there was more.

Betraying the 20-something bachelor-pad stereotypes, Luke's apartment didn't have bare walls. He didn't have a framed movie poster or an enlarged black-and-white nude photograph, either. He didn't have a poster of a supermodel in a bikini or one of those giant Fathead sticky posters of some athlete dunking a basketball or straight-arming a defender while fighting for a few more yards of Luke's living room. Luke knew enough about bachelor-pad chic to avoid things like ninja stars on the walls. He did have a few touristy trinkets. A ceramic sculpture of some Dia de los Muertos masks hung on his wall in the dinette above the table and chairs he'd picked up at Fred Meyer's. But on either side of that he'd positioned two framed photos, one of the four college friends who'd accompanied him on the trip to Mexico, and one a shot of a Maya temple he was particularly proud of, just to make sure visitors wouldn't think the skulls were part of some angst-y teenage death worship. The wall behind his TV held four framed pictures. The first was a shot of his parents on a backpacking trip. The second was a studio shot of his brother, sister-in-law and their baby, and the third was a matching larger shot of his infant niece from the same sitting. The fourth was a picture of his childhood home in New Orleans with the pre-Katrina roof. He accepted the new roof, and hardly had anything to complain about since the house had weathered the storm so well (and wasn't in the ninth ward so it hadn't flooded at all) but the old roof, with the mossy dark brown wooden shingles, felt more like his childhood: happier and more alive and less utilitarian and safe.

Balled up on one side of Luke's couch was the afghan blanket his mother had given him. On his coffee table, he'd put out classy coasters, even though he preferred the kind he stole from bars. And as he stepped into his kitchen and set his groceries on the marble countertop, he noticed the dusting of flour he'd missed when cleaning up from the batch of cookies he'd made himself the other day. All in all, it was not the house of a swinging bachelor, but of a lonely man in need of a wife, or at least a gay roommate who would appreciate his décor, gently suggest ways of improving it, and help him eat the excessive amount of cookies in the Tupperware container next to the fridge.

Ixtab saw all this, too. She stood in the living room, next to his TV, leaning her head against the wall because her headdress was frickin' heavy. She'd once been the Maya goddess of suicide, but as that empire had waned she'd been demoted down to the goddess of writers and journalists. Still, she liked a good suicide, if she could manage it. To her mind, a good suicide wasn't the act of some middle-aged accountant suffering from depression and buried in gambling debts, or the impulsive act of a pimply teenager who fully expected to attend his own funeral and enjoy watching the pretty girls cry over his corpse. No, she wanted artistry, and since she was basically limited to writers and journalists, when she wasn't persuading some famous and successful investigative reporter to commit obvious plagiarism, ruin his career, and send himself into a highly documented tailspin of blame and apologies on the blogosphere before offing himself, she was working on duping some truly promising novelist into hitting the big time and then putting the final punctuation on the book with a really dramatic bit of terminal self-harm. Devereaux served as a work in progress toward this end. She felt she could squeeze a truly great book out of him and make his life unbearable at the same time. So far, her most successful tactic had been his newfound position at Western Oregon University. Any big move takes a psychological toll, but for a Cajun boy who struggled to make a home for himself in New York City, the transition to a small town in the Northwest was particularly difficult. The isolation brought on by the lure of a tenure-track job in the midst of a particularly bleak economy had pushed Devereaux further inside himself and deeper into the novel he was writing. She thought she could get a good book out of him just before he'd had enough.

And it was going to be a good book. Perhaps even a great one. It had the scope of Tolstoy, covering a family that spanned from the Civil War, through segregation and Civil Rights, to 9/11 in New York and Katrina in New Orleans. Because Devereaux was a product of both worlds, he could capture the places in a way some hack from the young, peaceful, and drama-free Northwest never could. But despite the book's pastoral cast of characters and lush historical backdrop, Devereaux managed to play with the form, dancing and tiptoeing through time, shifting not only between pitch-perfect voices, but also between styles, sometimes writing about the Civil War like a blogger or even a series of twitter posts, sometimes writing about 9/11 like an African-American Southern Baptist civil rights crusader railing against injustice. It was a bit American-centric for her taste, but she couldn't fault a Roman for writing about Rome, and wouldn't have criticized a Mayan for writing a Maya-centric novel, if they'd had novels.

Ixtab straightened her headdress. It was a simple cap, not large enough to balance the weight of the large arc of feathers that sat on a spindle in the middle and curved in either direction wider than her shoulders. She carefully twisted her wide nose piercing into its proper place. The carved bone was pointy at both ends, for easy insertion, but the central point was a bit curved, and tended to make the bone arc away from her face, rather than toward her cheeks as it was supposed to. She was amazingly attractive, by Maya standards, thin but with wide hips and a heaving bosom, a wide, large nose, and a brilliant smile she could flash like a Cheshire cat's in the darkness of her smooth skin. Her eyebrows were a bit too pronounced for Maya physical perfection, but then they made her look serious, and it would have been unseemly for a goddess of suicide to look too cheerful.

She'd chosen to remain invisible to Devereaux, at least for now. There might come a time when she could safely reveal herself, perhaps even be physically intimate with her pet project, but she'd have to wait until he'd sunk deep enough into madness that he could safely write about her without revealing her to the other writers and journalists she'd be working on in the future. Those kinds of people tended to do research, and the last thing she wanted was to finally reveal herself to some reporter only to be instantly identified and then interviewed.

She stepped into the kitchen and stood so close to Devereaux that the feathers of her headdress brushed his face while he moved around, putting away his groceries. He couldn't feel the feathers, but each tickle made him want to go into his study and hammer out a few more words on his laptop. Somewhere in his brain, images of nooses and pills, pistols and long falls lodged themselves in crevasses that would only be plumbed in dark dreams.

Devereaux followed his implanted impulses back into the study where he opened his computer and ran a finger over the touch mouse, waking the machine. The screen glowed on, a Word document open with a taskbar full of documents lining the bottom of the image.

He scrolled down to the bottom of the current chapter, remembering his place in the narrative. This particular chapter was about a white high school teacher in New York who had survived 9/11 but was now grappling with the zeitgeist that seemed, to him, to be saying that all the problems of public education were the fault of bad teachers who couldn't get standardized test scores to rise. Since the teacher lived and breathed in a world of education, this felt like the country was blaming all the problems of the world at large on him. This mirrored the previous chapter about a man who, unbeknownst to the teacher, his second cousin. This man, an African American cop in New Orleans, lived in a world of criminals, and so when he watched the criminals losing all respect for law enforcement, he, too, felt that the center could not hold, the falcon could not find the falconer, and everything was turning and turning in the widening gyre. Devereaux actually considered putting some reference to the Yeats poem into his novel, perhaps from the mouth of the high school English teacher, but decided that was the kind of lame ploy that would only come to mind to the worst kind of hack. Though he knew he was disciplined enough to cut such a thing in the editing phase, he chided himself for even considering it.

Ixtab, standing over his shoulder, smiled at both his choice to omit something so cloyingly faux-literary, and his anguish in the process. Yes, she could make this man do himself in. And it was nice to see that he would go to such lengths to avoid anything cliché or too clever by half. No, his means of suicide, like his writing, would be meticulously devised and glorious in its execution. Though she knew it was a ways off, she felt a hum of excitement vibrating in her lower spine. She decided it was time to kick it into a higher gear.

Ixtab leaned forward very slowly and cocked her head so that her feathered headdress wouldn't brush against Devereaux's hair. She placed her lips centimeters from his ear. The whisper breathed out so silently that he couldn't distinguish it from his own thoughts. "Maybe the teacher should have an affair with a married woman."

Devereaux blinked, then leaned back in his chair so quickly that Ixtab had to jump out of the way. He made a hard "Poof" sound as he exhaled, then drew a long, slow breath through his nose. He knew the teacher, like the cop and his father, the judge, and his mother, the civil rights worker, and her father, the slave, and her mother, the slave nanny who was raped and sired the line that led to the New York teacher... they were all

Luke Devereaux. Every one of them was inside of him, a wriggling mass of genetic memory, geographic locations, political persuasions, personality defects, character flaws, and strange ticks. People would someday ask him which character he most identified with, or perhaps they would assume that he was most like the English teacher. After all, he taught writing at the college level. It wasn't such a leap. But they were all him. He would say so, if asked, and sound like a pretentious prick, but it was the truth. Every character in a book is a part of the author, whether she likes to admit it or not. And so, if his character was considering it, maybe he was, too. There was just no way around it.

Ixtab listened to his thoughts and realized she could have given the same advice about some character long ago, to the same effect. She'd made the same mistake as his hypothetical interviewer, thinking only the English teacher was a cypher for Devereaux. She hit herself in the forehead with the heel of her hand, then caught her headdress as it tumbled in front of her face. If she'd realized that he was all of the characters, he and that woman he'd been eying would probably be bonking their way toward two ruined lives and his hastened suicide by now. Dammit! she thought.

Devereaux thought about Christy. First he pictured her naked. He didn't like that he did this, but it always seemed to be the first image that came to mind. He literally shook his head, clearing the thought. Then he envisioned Christy dressed and carrying a stack of papers, then quickly looking away from his eyes at a department meeting. It took him a second but he managed to think of her in the abstract. She was married. That should be enough, he thought. It should all end there. She seemed happily married. That shouldn't be relevant, but it strengthened the case. She was happily married to a guy Devereaux had met, a guy who seemed nice, if a bit boring. Some kind of accountant or insurance salesman or something. What had his name been? Luke suddenly found himself obsessed with the need to remember her husband's name. He felt that, if only he could remember Christy's husband's name, the man would become more real, a hypothetical victim to the uncommitted crime he was considering. He knew the name had been something normal, something forgettable. Dammit, he thought.

Mr. Miller is enough, though, right? he thought. John Doe Miller? John Doe Miller didn't deserve to have his life ruined. And did Luke really intend to make Mrs. Miller into Mrs. Devereaux? And she had a kid, too, right? Luke certainly didn't want to take Mr. Miller's son and make him into Little Mr. Devereaux.

But, of course, that didn't have to be the consequence of an affair. Devereaux assured himself that he could be honest with Christy about his intentions. If she was looking for something he couldn't give, the whole issue would be moot, and he wouldn't have to worry about it anymore. He wouldn't have to think about her when he didn't want to, wouldn't have to see visions of her, undressed and beckoning him, when he wanted to be thinking about other things. Sure, it would make things awkward, but weren't they already?

He knew this was an oversimplification. A quick scan of his own book would teach the most casual reader that life is never so simple or straightforward, even when it was laid out in a more conveniently linear fashion. Life would get messy. Lies would become ugly revelations. Simple truths would become insults. But maybe she would just say no, and it could all go away.

Or maybe she wouldn't, he thought.

Ixtab smiled again.

15

The Inca had called him Ekkeko, and he went by that name in The City of God because it was easier for most people to remember, but when he wore his best clothes and skin, he really felt his Japanese name, Daikokuten, fit better. As he stepped out of the tunnel leading into the main room of Bacchanalia, the god of wealth turned heads in his black suit with the almost imperceptible gray pin stripes that matched those on his white shirt. This hint of gray accented the silver diagonal lines on the bright purple tie. This, in turn, pointed to the purple amethysts set in his square gold cufflinks, earrings, and the face of his gold watch. And this gold matched his skin, which wasn't like human skin painted with gold leaf, with all its texture. Instead, Ekkeko's flesh was as smooth as the shiniest idol. Even Ekkeko's features matched stylishly. His hard pressed mouth, bent in a jaunty sneer, matched the bend in his thin black eyebrows. His thick black hair, slicked back into a solid, reflective helmet, contained individual threads of silver that matched his tie. The only things that were simple about his perfect attire were his shoes, and they looked simply, perfectly fucking expensive.

Apart from his gold skin, Ekkeko had only one feature that was distinctly inhuman. His right hand, though fully functional, could not be seen. It wasn't transparent and reflective, like glass. He had a completely invisible hand. He wore golden rings on all his ten fingers, but the five on his right seemed to float where fingers should be.

Following Ekkeko closely, Enlil, god of air and political discourse, whispered incessantly in his ear about the identities of the people in the room, their particular social stations, and their usefulness. Much of this was lost on Ekkeko, who saw them all as poor and servile. That wasn't so bad. A lot better than poor and happy, but not quite as good as poor and jealous. He turned to one of these servants, an angel who provided some secondary level of security at this end of the tunnel.

"The best table you have," he said. "Highly visible but clearly exclusive." He put his visible left hand out as though he wanted to shake, but when the angel reached forward Ekkeko set cash in his hand but did not press it.

The angel, another of the large, gray, winged and clawed variety that made up most of Yahweh's security forces as well as private security guards for gods like Bacchus, took the bills and slid them inside the cloak of wings that wrapped around his body. He touched an earpiece and spoke some mumbled and possibly coded message into the cuff of his shirt, then said, "Right this way, sir."

Ekkeko found this satisfactory. As he walked around the round main stage he caught the eye of his favorite dancer, a woman who'd renamed herself Strawbari, misspelled in that tacky way Ekkeko loved. A woman taking on a humiliating spelling to her name was as erotic, in his opinion, as a woman taking a load in the eye. Strawbari saw him, smiled and winked, and then spun around her pole. Hooking one leg around it, she bent backward until she rested her hands on the floor and her bleached hair hung straight down from her upside-down head. Then she pushed her lips forward in a kiss aimed at him.

Behind Ekkeko, his best friend Horus, god of politicians and kings, shook patrons' hands as he made his way around the bar. Enlil stepped over to the bar and whispered in the bartender's ear. The bartender replied, and then Enlil went on whispering, and continued interrogating the man while cocktail waitresses brought the drinks he'd ordered, first a boilermaker for Horus, then a glass of 60-year-old single malt Macallan Scotch for Ekkeko. Horus loved his boilermakers because they were showy. The train of men had already gone from four to three, but as Ekkeko followed the angel the party diminished further because Horus stopped at a full table, set down his beer and the shot glass, introduced himself to the table's occupants, and then made a spectacle of dropping the shot in the beer and downing the whole thing to the cheers of his new friends. Ekkeko didn't turn to watch, and he didn't slow down. His friends would catch up. After all, he was the one buying.

A third of the way around the main stage, Ekkeko felt Strawbari slip her arm into his. "Daikokuten," she said, "what kind of services are you in the mood for this evening?"

He didn't look at her. "Careful, slut. Increased supply leads to lower demand."

Strawbari smiled. "I'm a luxury good, baby. Increased price leads to increased demand."

That earned both a look and a smile. Strawbari watched Ekkeko's thin lips part to reveal his gold teeth which were set in perfectly normal, pink gums. Then he licked his lips with his thick, wet, pink tongue. Strawbari was reminded that, for all his attention to detail on the outside, Ekkeko didn't stand up to too much close inspection.

"Oh, I'll probably be in the mood for something particularly expensive later this evening, my dear," he said.

She knew what that meant. Particularly humiliating. That was his kink. She tried her best to mask her repugnance with an eager smile. Ekkeko read both the revulsion in her eyes and the greed in that fake smile, and felt turned on by the juxtaposition. He reached around behind her and grabbed a meaty handful of ass, pulling her against his hip. Then he turned toward her slightly so he could raise his leg hard into her crotch.

This meant his back was turned when he heard the voice. He identified the word "ἔχιδνα," Greek for "viper." He also placed the accent. Aramaic. First century. Both these accomplishments led to the third; a swelling of pride. He managed all three of these tasks in an inhuman seven-tenths of a second. Ekkeko was good at feeling pride quickly. Unfortunately, he could not command his body to move as fast as he could inflate his self-concept, so he was only halfway through his rotation toward the speaker when an unidentified brown blur passed just beneath his right eye and smashed into his nose and upper lip.

Pinned between the thighs of the startled Strawbari and standing on one foot, at the point of impact he lost contact with the ground and sent Strawbari into a spin as he bounced off her shoulder and flew straight back against a small table for two behind him. For a second he registered that he'd found some safe, stationary position when the table rose to meet the angle of his back, but when the table continued to fall he sat heavily and banged the back of his head against his former means of support. Because he winced at this and closed his eyes, he still hadn't identified Jesus when the second punch caught him squarely in his left eye. His head clapped against the tabletop a second time.

Quite suddenly, Ekkeko had transformed from someone who could identify obscure accents to someone who couldn't even figure out which of his faculties were most compromised. He couldn't see properly. His hearing also seemed to be failing him, because after the stripper's scream, a hush had fallen over the room. Now he was hearing all kinds of incomprehensible shouting. He looked up just in time to see Jesus, Yahweh's Son, the one he always thought of as "that little socialist shit," drive his elbow into Enlil's face. Ekkeko's ears registered the sound of Enlil's nose breaking, but he couldn't comprehend that, either. And then chairs and tables were slamming into the ground as a bunch of other gods ran up behind Jesus. A couple of them wrapped large arms around the little Galilean. Was that Apollo and Baldur? Ekkeko didn't understand.

Now Horus was bellowing something, and he seemed to be squaring off with Thor, who towered over them all. Horus was shouting about how he would bury the boy, which was an odd turn of phrase for one immortal to choose when talking to another. Ekkeko leaned forward and tried to get up, then fell back. Out of his good eye, he saw a flash of light in Horus' direction. What was that?

The item Ekkeko couldn't identify was a sword in Horus' hand. He'd pulled the ornate, civil war style cutlass out of some pocket dimension. Now he was holding it up in front of Thor. The Norse god wasn't backing away.

Thor turned one shoulder in Horus' direction. Ekkeko could see what Horus couldn't; Thor was fiddling with the strap on his hammer, which was attached to his back hip. "It's to arms then? I honor your choice of style of combat, but methinks you have erred!" Now the hammer was in Thor's hand. The big Norseman made a tiny circular motion with the heavy rectangular head of the weapon no man could lift, then swung it around his body. Mjöllnir smashed into Horus' hand. All five of Horus' fingers were pulverized and his wrist broke as well. The fancy sword seemed to disappear. Then it reappeared, embedded halfway to the hilt in the far wall, 15 feet off the ground. Horus grabbed his crushed forearm but looked after his sword, so he didn't watch Thor bring the hammer around for a backhand blow that landed square in Horus' chest. The god of kings and politicians sailed up over Ekkeko, above the main stage, and fell into a cluster of small tables on the opposite side of the room.

Thor was looking after the god he'd launched into the air. Apollo, Baldur, Hephaestus, Sobek, Artemis, and Khepri were all busy trying to separate Jesus and Enlil. Ekkeko noticed that the little socialist shit was still struggling, but Enlil, though leaning forward, was mostly just shouting at this point. Ekkeko realized that no one was looking at him anymore. Despite his earlier struggles, he had no difficulty clambering up into a crouching position and launching himself at Jesus. He reached out, trying to grab at Jesus with his invisible hand. Unfortunately, someone (was that Sobek? It did smell a bit like algae) stuck out a forearm to ward him off, and he ran straight into it. The unidentified god's fist smashed into his other eye socket. Jesus, noticing this new attack, kicked out one leg, driving his toe into Ekkeko's stomach. Ekkeko made the exact opposite of a choking sound, something between a cough and a bark, and found that all the air had left his lungs.

Blind, mute, and choking, he couldn't comprehend the input from his remaining senses. Dozens of clawed hands were now wrapping around his legs and arms, lifting him off the ground. The booming voice of Bacchus, always jovial even when delivering orders, shouted something about throwing them all out. Then he felt himself lifted and carried. This was only a function of his inner ear and the wind from so many beating wings flowing over his gold skin.

And then the clawed hands were gone, and the wind changed. He was flying, his conventional means of travel, so this caused no panic, despite the fact that his eyes were closed. Ekkeko was more concerned with recovering his breath, so he found it a complete surprise when his flight took a parabolic turn and he slammed into the gold pavement of the Bacchanalia parking lot. He lay there scowling, and it took a long time for the full realization to set in; he'd just had his ass kicked by that little socialist shit.

Apollo and Baldur came out of the club on their own two feet. Though they were surrounded by security angels and mostly concerned with Jesus struggling against their grip, they managed to keep him between them and Ekkeko. Baldur watched as Thor was pushed out of the club (also still on his own two feet) and shook off the hands of the angels as he left the club's front doors. "Get thy hands off me!" Thor shouted. The angels positioned themselves to fight with him some more, but they didn't dare touch him again.

Then Baldur turned to Apollo, who nodded in the direction of Ekkeko. Both noted his position and carefully glided Jesus away. Artemis walked backward in front of Jesus, drawing his attention away by grabbing him by both shoulders and shouting, "Jesus, that was rad!" Apollo smiled at this. His sister was on an '80's slang kick lately.

Baldur elbowed Apollo gently as the crowd of angels dispersed and receded back into the club. Both gods slowed and let Hepehstus, Sobek, Artemis, and Khepri lead Jesus away. They listened as their friends rehashed the fight. Behind them, Enlil and Horus were lifting Ekkeko up. Though Horus was certainly the most seriously injured, his broken ribs and sternum were hidden by his clothing, and his smashed hand hung inconspicuously at his side, so Ekkeko, with blood running from his nose and split upper lip, and sporting puffy rings under both eyes that were starting to match the purple of his tie, looked the most defeated.

"What the hell was that all about?" Ekkeko shouted toward Baldur and Apollo.

"It could be that he knows you've all been sleeping with his wife," Apollo said.

"No. Methinks it's personal, Ekkeko," Baldur said. "He's always hated you." Both gods laughed.

Horus, Enlil, and Ekkeko rose up into the air and started floating off, but Ekkeko looked back over his shoulder and shouted, "You little socialist shit!"

Baldur and Apollo looked over to the ring of gods, to see if Jesus would lose it again. Instead, a dark hand rose up from among the taller gods, and Jesus calmly flipped off Ekkeko.

Apollo and Baldur laughed again, then turned toward one another. "Well, that was fun," Baldur said.

"Agreed," Apollo said, "but I'm still not convinced Jesus is taking his situation with Inanna seriously enough."

"Interested in doing a bit of sleuthing with me?" Baldur asked.

"I think that would be wise. Let's allow Jesus to enjoy his new-found freedom until we have something tangible to report."

The plan settled, the two wandered back to their friends to continue the night's festivities.

16

Sitting between The Linen Warehouse on its right and a karate dojo and tattoo parlor on its left, Andy's Café was tucked into a thin slot on Independence' Main Street. "Andy's Café" was painted on its front window in block letters. Inside, five booths lined one wall. Three tables sat along the other in the front of the café, followed by the short bar with only four stools. The kitchen was visible through a doorway with no door and an open window above the cash register. Three large whiteboards decorated the back wall, advertising: "Pies: $2.00 a slice. Strawberry Rhubarb, Dutch Apple, Pecan, Ala Mode – No Charge!" and "We have Ice Cream! Milk shakes! Malts! 24+ Flavors!" and, in smaller writing, "Specials... Pot Roast &

Eggs w/ hashbrowns and toast $11.95, Bacon Waffle & Eggs $6.25, Chicken & Dumplings!!! Soups."

Behind the bar, three framed pictures showed the serious faces of Marines in uniform, and another four unframed photographs showed four other men from the community in camouflage fatigues. Six of the men had served in Iraq or Afghanistan. The seventh was awaiting orders, and Yahweh knew the young soldier would be deployed to the Hindu Kush Mountains of Logar Province along the Afghanistan-Pakistan border by Christmas.

Under a small wooden shelf covered by 11 small bottles of Tabasco, soy sauce, Worcestershire and the like, more tacked-up photos presented kids ranging from toddlers to pre-teens sporting Oregon Beavers gear. Another framed picture, this one black and white, showed four men in aprons, arms draped over one another's shoulders, above a brightly colored label that read, "Family Feud: Beavers/Ducks" in the Beavers' orange and black and the Ducks' green and yellow.

The opposite wall, behind the booths, held six framed black and white photos of things like the rolling fields of grass seed around the town, or buildings at the Western Oregon University campus shot from interesting angles.

The only thing about Andy's that was intentionally old-fashioned was a decorative clock hanging on the wall near the entrance to the kitchen, and that could have been purchased at Target or Pier One anytime. But the fresh coat of mauve paint on the walls seemed to cover something much older. Sure, the aging wood paneling could have decorated the café 50 years earlier, long before it became "Andy's." He'd only owned the place for 14 years, but he'd seen a picture of it from 1944. Still, something about the comfortable atmosphere, the soft light rippling under the slow moving ceiling fan, the sizzle whispering out of the kitchen, the echoes of laughter and conversation that lingered long after the patrons left each night, would make a person wonder: What was behind that fresh coat of paint? If you could scrape off the years along with the paint and the walls, would you find the spot where Nez Perce congregated to cook the steelhead they caught in the Willamette River nearby? And did the predecessors of the Incas stop in this very spot as they made their way to South America ten thousand years ago? Inside Andy's Café that felt more than just possible. It felt likely.

Of course, to Yaheweh, it was an un-romantic certainty. But that wasn't why He'd chosen to come to Andy's every week. He liked the coffee, and Andy made a hell of a Denver omelet if Yahweh ever felt bored with His kosher diet.

The fork didn't know this, though. That's not a criticism. It was a fork. It lay on a paper napkin next to Joe's coffee cup. Denise always set out silverware as a way of encouraging patrons to buy some food to go with their coffee, but Joe and Manny never took the bait, so the fork had the early morning shift off, as it did during all Joe and Manny's weekly meetings.

"So, this Inanna is up to something?" Joe asked.

"She's making a play. I need to figure out her next move, because the first one was pretty weak. Below her capacity. It's got to be a part of something larger."

Joe rested his hand on the countertop. The fork found itself under the tip of his middle finger.

"What does Frigga think? Have you talked with her about it?"

Yahweh shook his head. "My wife doesn't like to talk politics. I mean, she'll share country-club gossip, but when it gets important, she …demurs."

Joe looked down at his coffee. "My wife loves talking politics. It's her way of avoiding more important subjects."

"Hmm." God frowned.

Joe traced the handle of the fork with his finger. The fork couldn't feel the soft skin dance down the slightly raised ridge that ran along his handle, a handle far too ornate for coffee-shop silverware. Paisley shapes with curly-cue ends twisted against the edge of the handle, and in the midst of this filigree there was even a small hole that showed the countertop below. Something like a squashed fleur-de-lis or a club from a deck of cards finished of the fork's handle. The fork allowed Joe to trace his finger from this decoration all the way back up the ridge to the other end of the handle, nearest his tines. The fork let Joe lift it up and feel his heft, also unusual for coffee-shop fare. If Joe had looked more closely, he might have noticed that the fork was made of silver.

Tarnish darkened the spaces between the tines and smudged the creases in the decorative curls of the handle. Andy had purchased the fork at an estate sale, a forgotten piece of a broken set that came to a couple as a wedding gift, lived most of its life in a velvet-lined box at the back of a cupboard, and didn't long survive its owners' demise. This orphan fork found his new family in a drawer full of un-matching silverware behind Andy's counter. The fork had never commented on the fact that Denise always reached for him when setting the place for Joe and Manny. Perhaps it was unconscious on Denise's part. Perhaps, in some deep recess of her brain, she recognized the weight of the fork, or the unusual hole in the crest, and identified this fork as special. Sometimes the fork would go to Manny, and sometimes to Joe, but it always found its way onto the counter for their weekly meetings.

The fork didn't respond when Joe scratched the tips of his fingers against the ends of the fork's tines.

"So, I guess I don't understand," Joe said.

"What?"

"Well, you know everything, right? So why does this make you nervous?"

Yahweh snorted. "Omniscience is a little more complicated than you might expect. I don't know everything, in the sense that you know what you had for dinner last night, or the name of that actor in that movie you saw last Saturday. I have access to knowledge of all the possibilities, all the things that could happen, could be happening, could have happened."

"So, it's like Wikipedia for the future, but with pages for every possibility?"

"Sort of. But also the present and the past. And I know every probability."

This was far too complicated for the fork to grasp.

"So, what's Inanna most likely going to do?"

"She's a deity, too, remember. She knows the odds. She'll choose something I'm unlikely to catch, but which she calculates is likely to work. But I make it sound like it's all math. A lot of it's just hunches and will."

"Well, what are the odds that you'll still be top dog in a week, a month, and a year?"

Manny leaned back in his chair, far from Joe's fork. "You know how they use supercomputers to try to predict the stock market, but they can never account for all the variables? I can tell you the value of my stock with some accuracy for hours, a few days, but then it...," God made an exploding gesture with His hands, "...poofs into a giant probability cloud."

The fork allowed Joe to pick him up and toss him into the air, just less than a centimeter above Joe's hand. "Does all your knowledge of the future do that? Poof, I mean?" Joe asked.

"And the present. And the past. All probability clouds."

"Even the past isn't set in stone?"

"Even stone isn't stone. It most likely was stone, most likely is stone, and most likely will be stone until it wasn't, isn't, and won't be."

Joe set the fork down again, not on the soft napkin but on the countertop itself. The fork sang and vibrated against the counter and came to rest against the side of the coffee mug. "You lost me there," Joe said.

"The math becomes Zen, at a point."

Joe picked up his mug. The fork danced sideways when the mug bumped his raised chest. Joe sipped the coffee, then set the mug down again. This time the fork hid in the mug's shadow but wasn't touched by it.

"So," Joe hesitated, "my wife?"

Yahweh looked at Joe sideways, then pressed his lips together hard before speaking. "She's your wife until she wasn't, isn't, and won't be."

"That's what I'm worried about. Things feel... rocky."

The three of them sat in silence for a while. The fork was the most comfortable with this.

"Oh, I have some good news," Yahweh said.

"Yeah?"

"Jesus actually got out of the house the other day. He got together with some friends and went out to a club."

"A club?"

148

"Yeah," God said. "Bacchanalia, it's called. It's a strip club. Owned by Bacchus, the Greek god of wine and partying. Very hip right now."

Joe turned so fast in his seat that his hand bumped the fork into the coffee cup again. The fork shook with the force of Joe's surprise.

"Jesus went to a strip club?"

"Yup." Yahweh smiled.

"Dammit! Every time I think one of my teachers taught me something about religion or mythology that was actually right, you say something that just blows my misconceptions away."

Yahweh snorted. "Don't be too hard on your teachers. Your species hasn't even figured out how to use taukluthorium to make helioplasm yet."

Joe turned back to his coffee. "I don't even know what those things are."

"Exactly. Five hundred years ago your ancestors could have complained about their teachers, and I could have said your species couldn't even make a working helicopter. And five thousand years before that I could have said that your species hadn't figured out how to smelt silver yet."

The fork's ears would have perked up at this point, if it'd had any.

"And yet," God continued, "all the way back then, teachers were telling kids that they knew all about the gods. Now you wouldn't listen to some teacher tell you about the gods if they came from a tribe of hairless apes who couldn't even make that fork there." God pointed at the fork. Joe picked it up, as though it would help him understand God's point. The fork didn't mind being used as a prop in this way. "And you wouldn't listen to someone who didn't at least understand the basic principles that keep a helicopter in the air. So why would you believe that someone who doesn't know how to use taukluthorium to make helioplasm has all the answers about the nature of the gods?"

"Well, sure, I guess." Joe frowned. "But that hairless ape who couldn't make this fork could still teach a kid how to make a fire."

"And more power to him. And the kid should listen. But if the fork is more complicated than the fire, then why should the kid believe that early human explaining the magic of the helicopter? And if helioplasm synthesis is more complex than helicopters, don't you think the gods are a bit more complicated than anything your teachers could explain to you?"

Joe looked hard at the fork in his hand. "You're right. I can't even figure out how to maintain a marriage. Why do I expect myself to know whether Jesus is the kind of guy who goes to strip clubs owned by Greek gods?"

Yahweh sipped his coffee, then set it down slowly. "Maintaining a marriage can be more complex than smelting forks, making helicopters fly, or using taukluthorium to make helioplasm."

"So what should I do?" Joe asked.

"Go home and hug your son," Yahweh said. The fork did not know that Jesus had been tossed out of a bar for kicking Ekkeko's ass, so it couldn't understand that particular smile on God's face. "Hope he keeps making you proud." God stood and pulled his coat off the back of the seat.

"What does that have to do with my wife?"

Yahweh froze, then looked down at Joe, frowning. "You don't think your son has anything to do with your relationship with your wife? Joe, I know you're one of the smart ones, but sometimes your species is so dumb." He pulled his coat on and mumbled, "Hairless apes may never even get to helioplasm. Stupid...." God kept muttering to himself as he opened the door, dinging its bell, and stepped out onto the sidewalk.

Joe watched him go through the large storefront window and gripped the fork tightly. He couldn't deny his urge to stab God with the fork, though he knew he'd never do it.

17

Ghair Aadi watched the second take of the video on his laptop screen, then closed it in frustration. He grabbed a piece of three-hole-punched notebook paper from a plastic package of loose sheets, then started looking for a pen. Once he found it, he scribbled half a word, discovered that the pen wouldn't write, started scratching a tiny little circle which grew into a widening, ragged arc until the paper tore. He crumpled the sheet, threw it as hard as he could at the computer screen, then sank back in his chair and sighed.

"He's wise to try and write a script for himself before filming," Baldur said.

Apollo nodded. "Trying to do it off the cuff was leading to too many 'ahhs' and 'ums.'"

The two gods floated two stories above the Rue de Steinkerque, just outside the open window of Ghair Aadi's little apartment bedroom. Below them, tourists walked up and down the sloped street, heedless of the shadows they couldn't see. The gods were invisible, though not intangible, but no one on the street below noticed when a pigeon flew into Baldur's back, fell five feet in a daze, then flapped like mad as it recovered. In fact, no one but Baldur noticed that the startled bird evacuated its bowels on impact.

"Paris is filthy," the god said as he made a new pair of pants appear in place of the soiled ones.

Apollo nodded toward Ghair Aadi's lab equipment. "Pestilential."

Baldur didn't laugh. "How many people do you think his viral agents will kill?"

"Hard to say," Apollo replied. He leaned in toward the window and looked at the equipment for a moment. "Quite an impressive display of bioengineering, actually. Aerosolized Marburg virus. It doesn't exist in nature, as such, but the Marburg virus, from which this is derived, comes from the Lake Victoria region of Africa. It causes Marburg hemorrhagic fever, also known as green monkey disease."

Baldur nodded as though he knew this already, but, truly, medicine had never been his strongest area of study.

Apollo barely noticed his friend. He was on a nerd splurge. "The infected get symptoms they may ignore at first. Headaches and fever, mostly. Then, after five days, they start to get a nasty rash. Then weight loss, pancreatitis, jaundice. Some will suffer neuropsychiatric symptoms, others will hemorrhage both internally and externally. Most of those who die will succumb to organ failure, usually of the liver. Lethality can range from 23 to 90 percent. I don't know how much his aerosolization will affect lethality, so it could be anywhere in that range." The god shrugged. "Of course, if the death toll from the disease reaches a certain point, public services shut down, including things like plumbing, and you get outbreaks of cholera and the like."

"Of course," Baldur said.

"Also, there will be panic, and many will die in the looting and the government crackdown. If it's really bad, governments will try to control outbreaks through slash and burn strategies in hotspots. Because some people do heal, this won't kill everyone in the world. But…," Apollo looked at Baldur, "if he managed to kill a quarter the people in the world, I wouldn't be completely surprised."

"Forsooth?" Baldur shook his head while he did his own math. "This man could kill two billion people?"

Apollo nodded. "Maybe a lot more."

"So, what's the video for?"

Apollo looked back at Ghair Aadi. The man was looking at the ceiling, blowing bubbles made of spit, then lifting them with carefully aimed exhalations. One fell on his forehead, and Ghair Aadi sat up suddenly, wiping the spit off his forehead and launching into a new burst of profanity in Farsi.

"He's going to claim the attack in the name of al Qaeda in Mesopotamia. But he's also going to mention that he's an Iranian. He will say he's doing this in the name of Islam. But he's not a Muslim. It's a lie. He's an atheist."

"Then why do it?"

"He thinks he's a schizophrenic. He wants to leave a mark on the world before he loses his mind. Plus, the voices are telling him to do it."

"Inanna and Toliq," Baldur said.

"Exactly."

"But why? What do they stand to gain?"

"The whole world, from the ashes," Apollo said. "They hope to start a world war between the Islamic world and the West."

"Which side do they expect to win?" Baldur asked.

"I'd bet they are expecting the West to win, but I also think they don't care. In either case, Inanna wants the winners to worship her. And Toliq, well…." he trailed off.

"What does she want?"

"She just wants them to stop thinking. To detest knowledge itself. To hate the science, engineering, and intellect that made something like—" he pointed at the machinery on Ghair Aadi's lab table "—that possible."

"It's a pretty compelling case," Baldur said.

Apollo turned on him suddenly. "You don't mean that!"

Baldur frowned. "My friend, you are the god of light and music and reason. Our jurisdictions overlap, if not our provenance. But I concern myself not only with light and beauty, but also with love and happiness. I admit that Toliq's world of primitives struggling to survive would have less light and less beauty. But if your reason can create weapons that can kill billions of people, what does that say about its ability to produce greater love and happiness?"

Apollo was astounded. "Do you really think there would be more love and happiness in Toliq and Inanna's world? That…well, that just doesn't make any sense."

"Not at first, sure. There would be all kinds of horrors. But maybe your science has outstripped your sister Athena's wisdom. Maybe what they can do has replaced what they should do, and that's why so many have lost sight of how to be happy."

Apollo turned back toward Ghair Aadi and shook his head. "No. That's wrong. It's not a failure of reason that creates a man like this one. It's the hatred of reason. It's a vacuum of knowledge created by those who wish to fill that space with their own poison. Look at the way Toliq and Inanna have manipulated him. They didn't tell him the truth. They didn't make some persuasive argument that the only way this atheist would have some legacy would be to wipe out a quarter of the humans on the globe. They lied to him. They pretended to be voices in his head, the disembodied personifications of irrationality itself. He accepted his own madness, but that's only an extreme example of so many kinds of denial. He refused to think, and chose to believe. It wasn't that reason failed. It was a failure of light. Our failure. Yours and mine. We allowed too much darkness, too much self-deception. And Toliq feeds on that. And Inanna saw Toliq's growing power and is trying to turn it to her own use."

Then he almost whispered. "I'm not even sure she can control Toliq. Inanna's lust for power is insatiable, so she will try anything, but I think she may find Toliq's kind of intentional stupidity to be an unconquerable force. They may worship Inanna for a while, but eventually they will forget how to worship. There will be no light or music in Toliq's world, Baldur, but there will be no beauty or love or happiness either, because even these require thought." He turned back to his friend. "You know that to be true. Happiness, real happiness, is the product of intentionality, and love is the product of will. Beauty is the product of intellect. These things aren't accidents. That's why we are not the first causes, we're not the early gods. We are the children of gods, because something must come before beauty and happiness and love. I may not like Yahweh too much. He is a simple builder god, a god of might and will, creation and management, but He sustains us just as He sustains His creation, and we can fill it with light and music and happiness and love. If we stand up to Toliq."

Now it was Baldur's turn to nod. "Methinks you have gained some of your sister's wisdom. I am convinced." He put his hand on Apollo's shoulder. "I make this covenant with you: We shall stand against Toliq together."

They hovered in silence for a moment, watching Ghair Aadi. The unusual Iranian Arab was now crumpling up sheets of paper into little balls, then shooting them, basketball style, in high arcs that landed behind his laptop.

"So," Baldur asked, "if we stand against Toliq, does that mean we will side with Jesus against Inanna?"

Apollo frowned. "I suppose. At least temporarily. But his love, is it really enough?"

Baldur looked over at his friend. "What do you mean?"

"Well, it seems to me, you have love covered, but between the two of us, we have a lot to add to that. Light and music and reason come to mind."

"His Christians are pretty good at the light and music."

"They also have quite an organization. But I think they could benefit from a bit more reason."

"So what are you suggesting?"

Apollo shrugged. "Maybe it's too early to say. Jesus is my friend, and I wouldn't want to betray him. I know he's your step-brother and your friend, too. But if Inanna were to be taken down along with Toliq, it might create some room for someone who still wanted something to do with Jesus' followers. I'm not convinced he has that much interest in them anymore. And if we had them, and we could fill the world with light and beauty and music, maybe Yahweh would decide to take your mother's advice and just retire. And then...well, who knows?"

Baldur nodded. "Methinks thine drift is clear, if a bit premature. First, we'll need to tell Jesus and my brother Thor what we've found. Your sister will be on our side, certainly. She hates Inanna . We have some conversations to arrange."

"Agreed," Apollo said.

Unbeknownst to the two gods, their covenant was not without a witness. The tourists on the street couldn't see the floating gods above them, and Ghair Aadi could look out his window and only see the dome of the Basilique du Sacre Coeur. But above them all, floating four stories over the streets of Paris, another god watched.

Meme spied on the gods who spied on his precious Ghair Aadi. He loved Aadi's inherent irony. Meme was rooting for Ghair Aadi's success even though he was in constant conflict with Inanna and Toliq. Between you and me and a lamppost, he hated Toliq's conscious ignorance and viewed Inanna's Church as the institution of the opposition. But he also believed that the religious war her protégé would cause would ultimately lead to the end of all religious devotion. You can't make an omelet without breaking a few eggs. If it seems ironic that a god would want humans to be atheists, that was perfectly fine with the god of post-modernity, who actively denied his own existence and sneered at the stupidity of those who believed otherwise. He was caught between a rock and a hard place, and loved that almost as much as he loved the layers of a tired cliché.

Meme frowned, just a scrunching of his smooth eyebrow area. He wasn't sure quite what would happen when humans gave up on gods. Would he truly cease to exist? When you play with fire, you're gonna get burned. Or would he cease to be ironic and become only tragic? He wasn't sure, but he thought there was a good doctoral thesis in there somewhere.

Meme shook his featureless head. He realized he was putting the cart before the horse. He didn't want to count his chickens before they hatched. If Apollo and Baldur stopped Ghair Aadi, the philistines would not only go on believing in deities, but might even discover that they'd been saved by a pair of them. If so, he'd go back to being just a hipster god with a tiny cult following, and everyone knew those kinds of gods were douches. No, he realized, he was just going to have to bite the bullet and give Inanna a heads-up.

18

Christy came down the stairs and discovered that Joe had come home while she'd been up in their room, folding laundry. As she walked down the hallway, she could see his back and the back of his head above the couch. Next to him, half of Dawkins' head poked up.

She could hear the rhythmic, halting cadence of her son's reading. Clearly the book was difficult for him, and Joe had to help with a handful of words, but Dawkins plowed ahead like a 4X4 off-roading through the muddy text. Christy felt that familiar tightening in her chest; her son's exceptional reading ability always made her particularly proud. She supposed this was how athletic parents felt when their children excelled at sports. As a literature and writing professor, the written word was her game, and Dawkins' success at it tugged at that particular genetic heartstring in the DNA that sings out "This child really is your offspring."

With that chord still humming, her breath caught in her throat when Joe turned to look at her. Dawkins' other half, the man who'd given her son his defiant double cowlick, his tall, thin frame, and toes that perfectly matched his father's, now turned to look at her with an expression she couldn't easily sum up. The smile on his face, tight and hard, spoke of the same pride she felt in Dawkins. But his eyes, those generous gray-green eyes she'd wanted to stare at through the whole meal on their first date, now sent her some sad story. He blinked, and she saw it. It wasn't Romeo and Juliet, or even Othello. Othello might have made her defensive. After all, she hadn't done anything with Luke Devereaux. She'd only really spoken to Luke a few times. And Luke was no Iago. And, for that matter, Joe was no Othello, no war hero, no great leader of men. He was a fucking insurance salesman, for Chrissakes, she thought. He couldn't play that kind of jealous husband.

But he wasn't. That wasn't the look. When he blinked, she saw Lear, broken and holding onto Dawkins, his Cordelia, his good child, because his Goneril and Regan had broken his heart. Without the boy reading there on the couch, Joe would be ripping off his clothes and wandering around in the rain, raving like a lunatic who'd mastered iambic pentameter. And Christy knew which parts she was playing. She was Goneril and Regan, greedy and self-absorbed and disloyal, turning away from her husband for the dashing, ambitious young man who made her feel just a little bit younger and smarter and less like herself. And she knew that she would destroy her Lear, but she would destroy herself first. Goneril poisons Regan, then stabs herself. Christy would turn on herself, too. She could never live in the shadow of that look, in the spotlight of those wet eyes.

Joe's glance lasted only a few seconds. He tried to turn back to Dawkins without disturbing the reading, but Dawkins felt the turn, or maybe the shift in the temperature of the room, and stopped. He popped up onto his knees and looked over the back of the couch.

"Mommy! Daddy just got home. I'm reading him one of the new books from the book fair."

"Which one, honey?" she asked. She stepped into the kitchen and grabbed a glass from the cupboard next to the sink, then turned back and filled it with ice and water from the door of the refrigerator. She thought she knew the answer to her question, based on the little bit she'd heard Dawkins read, but she wasn't really listening to Dawkins' reply.

"Oh, good," she said. Then she took a big gulp of the cold water, sucking it through her teeth until they hurt.

"Christy?" Joe said. "Are you feeling okay?"

Bitterness flashed. Didn't he know? Hadn't he just accused her with a look? But she swallowed it down with the water. He didn't know. Not about Luke. He wasn't accusing. He was reaching out. And now he was worried about her physical health. He was confused and grasping, an aging ninth-century Celtic king whose empire was falling apart.

"I'm fine," she said. "I just realized I left something at work. I mean, at the store, I was going to get something on the way home. It's stupid, I just… I gotta go."

She tried not to run down the hall, and when she grabbed her coat off the hooks by the door she pulled so hard the little tag ripped off. Tears blurred her vision by the time she was trying to put the key in the car door, and once she was safely in her seat, her belt pulled on, her hands at ten and two, she let loose and sobbed, just once, before turning the key in the ignition and dropping the little automatic into reverse.

No god rode along with Christy as she cried in her car. As an atheist, she didn't expect any, but Meme, the god of atheism, did not find her worthy of his plans. Frigga, foremost goddess of wives and mothers, did not care much about Christy's future as Christy made her way out of their suburban cul-de-sac. She was not a politician, so Horus took no notice of her, and she only made a professor's salary, so Ekkeko couldn't have cared less. Jesus, occupied with the undoing of his own marriage, had no time for this crisis in Christy's. Toliq would have nothing to do with a college professor, and Inanna was busy with her schemes. Muhammad, a prophet rather than a god, tended to his goats. Ixtab was too focused on her tragic writer to keep an eye on this cog in his self-destruction. No one would have listened to Christy's prayers, even if she'd bothered to voice any. She was completely alone.

This is why the gods fail. Sometimes they do not pick us up and carry us down the beach. Sometimes they let us drive down the road, alone in our cars, sniffing up gobs of snot and self-loathing while we leave no footprints at all.

So it was amazing that Christy made it to her destination. She hadn't even known she had a particular destination. She'd just been trying to escape. Somehow, through her own tears and the light rain that spit on her windshield, she made out the road before her and followed it. She didn't turn on the radio. The damp weather, the dependable Oregon rain that makes for green fields, gray skies, and seasonal affective disorder, absorbed all the sound outside the car. Inside, the hum of the engine provided no comfort or direction, but she drove on, down Monmouth Avenue, through the S curves, through the main stoplight on Highway 99, past the turn for Western Oregon University. Then she made a left and entered a neighborhood of apartment buildings, many filled with college students, others with poor, working-class families. And then she made another left into a parking lot. And then she was standing at a door, wondering how she knew where he lived. Had someone told her? She wasn't that good with directions. Had she driven him home once? She would have remembered. So how had she known to come to this door? And what did she expect to do now that she was here?

Before she could decide what to do, she'd knocked. She frowned and looked at her knuckles, white from the impact.

When Luke opened the door, he stared at Christy without saying anything. Her blond hair was wet and streaked with brown. Her brow was scrunched in extravagant confusion. She was gaping at her own hand. "Christy?" He sounded like he wasn't even sure it was her, because, in fact, he wasn't.

Her head snapped up. "Um, yeah. Hey," she said.

He waited for her to explain the visit. She didn't. In the silence, he noticed she'd been crying.

"C'mon in," he said. "What's up? You look upset."

She stepped in the door. Now she was sure she'd never been here before. She looked around at the mostly bare white walls, the strange Mexican skulls over the dinette table, the 5x7s in frames on the entertainment center. The bare walls made the pictures look so small. She wanted to take the time to stare at them, to try to paint some picture of this man outside of work, but she already felt like an invader. "I'm fine," she said.

Luke didn't argue, but he knew enough to wait. She stood still in his living room and neither heard the sound of Ixtab's headdress falling off and bouncing on the linoleum in the kitchen as the goddess shook with excitement. Luke said, "Please, have a seat. Can I get you something to drink? I have beer and Coke and I think there's some Scotch somewhere here."

"A water would be great."

"Ice?"

"Please. My throat is scratchy."

Ixtab stepped out of his way as he entered the kitchenette, but she bounced on the balls of her feet behind him while he got ice out of the freezer. He brought Christy the ice water, then sat slowly on the edge of his recliner. The chair faced the TV, but he turned and rested his elbows on his knees so he could lean toward her. "So, what's going on?"

"Look, Luke, this is going to sound stupid." She took a deep breath. "No, it's going to sound crazy. Like I've lost my mind. And I feel as if I have." She set the glass of water down on his coffee table, leaned back, and pressed the heels of her hands into her eye sockets. "Oh goddamnit, I am so sorry."

"It's okay," Luke said. He wanted to say something else, anything else, but couldn't figure out where this was going.

Christy looked quickly at Luke. His eyes, those golden eyes, looked gentle, his lips soft. She decided not to keep looking at him. Instead, she leaned forward so she could stare down at her hands. This entailed placing her own elbows on her knees, a mirror of his pose, and it meant her hands were very close to his. She thought he might take her hands, just to comfort her, and that would be bad. Her fear made her speak more quickly. "Luke, look, this is going to sound like it's totally coming out of left field, and I know I'm blind-siding you with this, and it's not your fault and I'm sorry. I'm so sorry."

"It's fine—" he tried.

"But here's the thing," she interrupted. "I've felt like we need to talk about us."

Luke leaned back in his chair. "I hope I haven't done anything to...you know, crossed any lines or anything."

She risked a glance at him. "No, you haven't done anything wrong. I've just felt...I don't know, something. And that's a problem, not with you, but with me, because I'm happily married."

She'd said "happily" because if she'd just said "married" it might have sounded like she was going in a very different direction. But once she heard her own word double back on her ears, she wondered. She thought she was happy. But was Joe happy? He hadn't looked happily married tonight.

"I know," Luke was saying, "and I'd never want to, you know, come between anything."

"I know that. And you haven't done anything to, like...." She struggled. "You haven't done anything wrong. It's me. I'm a mess. I don't know what's wrong with me."

Ixtab, holding her heavy headdress in one hand, leaned down next to Luke and touched his face while she whispered in his ear. Though he didn't know that she spoke, or even existed, he knew the goddess' words were true; if he leaned forward now, he could take Christy's hands. And then he could comfort her with a side-hug on the couch. And then she'd cry, and he'd be holding her. And then she'd kiss him, desperately and angrily. And then they'd be muttering about how they shouldn't while they did. He could see the sequence of events, like a comic book made of grimy Polaroids or low-quality screen captures of an amateur porn movie made with a webcam. The comic book didn't have much of an ending, and pornography isn't known for its complete narrative arc. And that was the pivot point for him, the climax to his story, the moment of moral crisis. It wasn't about being the other man, about honoring the institution of marriage. Luke decided he had to be true to himself, not as a paragon of virtue, but as a writer. And as a writer, he couldn't choose to ignore the next part of the story. It would be so easy to think only of the scene, to forget the larger plot, to pretend it would work itself out or unfold in some organic way. But Luke refused to lie to himself. The story would continue after the last Polaroid, and it wasn't a novel in which he wanted to be a main character. Christy and whatever-her-husband's-name-was: this was their book. He was secondary. He didn't want to be the villain. At least not that kind of sleazy villain. This story was not for him.

"Christy," he said, "I could pretend I don't know what you're talking about. But you're not stupid. I've felt it, too. And I don't want to be that person. Not to you. I don't want to ruin your life. And I think it would be too weird for me to just pretend we haven't felt this way. Because I have. I've thought about it, too. And that's a problem for both of us. I mean, it says something about your marriage, but it says something about me, too." He didn't elaborate about his distinction between his moral character and his narrative one. "I've been thinking that Western isn't really a good fit for me. I have a friend at CUNY. They have an MFA in creative writing at Brooklyn College, and he thinks he might be able to get me an adjunct position there. It wouldn't be tenure track, but it gets me back to New York, and I've been thinking about it. I think

I need to do that. I think, you know, it would just be too weird if I stayed."

He waited for her to try to dissuade him.

She sniffled, nodded. "Yeah, that's probably best."

"Really?"

"Huh?"

Luke tilted his head like a curious golden retriever. "Well, I just thought you'd try to talk me out of it. I mean, I agree, that it's the best thing. But I thought you'd be like, 'Oh, no, I don't want to run you out of town.'"

Christy laughed at the silly voice he gave her, at his genuine smile, at her own relief. She wiped a tear out of her eye with a long sideways swipe. Then she dared to lay her hand on his, if only for a second. "I think I need to work on telling the truth more, not lying more. I am sorry if that means I'm running you out of town...."

"No, it's the best thing."

Ixtab's headdress started to slide to the side again. She reached up, grabbed it violently, slammed it down on Luke's floor with all her might, and stomped into the kitchen.

Christy could look at Luke again. "You're too big city for Monmouth anyway, Luke." She stood and started to leave.

"Maybe," he said as he rose. "But Christy?"

She turned back.

Ixtab leaned her head into the small livingroom.

Luke tilted his head and raised his eyebrows. "There's a lot to be said for small-town guys."

Ixtab rolled her eyes, then mimed gagging herself with a finger down her throat.

Christy nodded. "I'd better get back to my small-town guy."

She left. But when she turned the ignition key she sat in her car for a moment. She realized that when she'd said "my small-town guy," she'd meant Dawkins. Imagining the conversation with her other small-town guy filled her with a sharp dread.

19

Apollo and Baldur made their ascension to Asgard, really more of a trans-dimensional shift sideways and diagonally rather than up, and arrived in the void outside the floating mountains that held The City of God. As they floated toward Asgard, they continued making their plans in hushed tones. Far-seeing eyes watched their approach.

The pair of gods made their way over the island and into the suburbs of housing complexes for the dead. Between these vast towers, over the shining streets of gold, Baldur and Apollo saw their reflections in the mirrored windows, but could not see those who lay in wait for them.

"Methinks we should discuss our discovery with my brother Thor first. I know you'll be worried about his temper, but I promise you that if we assure him of an opportunity for great and righteous battle, he can be persuaded to be patient," Baldur said.

Apollo shook his head. "I think it would be safer to include Artemis first. If the three of us approach Thor we can assuage his concerns about Jesus' affinity for peaceful solutions and guarantee him that the four of us will see to it that there will be some bloodshed before the end of this matter."

Baldur shrugged. "Well, at least we agree that Jesus should be told last. He may seek to reconcile with his wife, or at least reason with her, and we would lose the element of surprise, which is our greatest asset at this point."

Suddenly Apollo threw out an arm and stopped his friend. The two hovered in place, Baldur looking at Apollo, Apollo listening.

"What is it?"

Apollo looked hard at Baldur. Then a sadness sunk into his eyes, the expression of a mortal learning he has been condemned. "My friend, we have already lost the element of surprise."

Shadows flashed from below them, cast by the light of the glowing streets. Because Asgard had no sun of its own, there was no warning of the multitude swarming above. Apollo and Baldur moved away from each other slightly and turned, back to back, as they examined the forces amassing around them.

A small army of hired seraphim, their 14 wings forming not seven pairs, or seven times seven, but seven times 77 pairs of dark grey, bat-like shadows flapping in great gusting bursts in a moving sphere, surrounded the gods. Through this fluttering mass of mercenary claws and teeth, five new figures floated into the globe. Apollo identified each one quickly, despite the background of moving darkness. Enlil, Horus, and Ekkeko took positions around and behind them. In front of them, Inanna and Toliq came to a stop just a few feet away.

"You are feeling very confident these days, Inanna," Apollo said.

"Quite a brazen hussy, methinks," added Baldur.

Inanna shrugged. "I've been called a lot worse."

"You will be once your plans are revealed," Apollo said.

"Ooo," Toliq cooed. "I like Revelations. I just don't like people learning new things."

Baldur blinked. "Apollo, you're the god of knowledge. Do you know where her stupidity ends and her madness begins?"

"No," Apollo said. "But Toliq proves that enough stupidity becomes insanity."

Toliq smiled at Inanna and spoke in a voice of candy-covered acid. "They are trying to insult me. That's what these elites do." She looked at Apollo. "You don't get it. My ignorance is the perfect defense against your words, god of knowledge. I refuse to understand what you are saying." She leaned forward and choked up a great gob of saliva, then spat at his feet. "See? You have no power over me."

"How about this?" Apollo thrust his hand toward Toliq. She dodged to the side as a blast of pure, white, hot light shot out of his palm. The wide beams sizzled the air like meat over a fire. Though the blast missed Toliq, it cut a line in the spinning sphere of angels who swarmed around them just by holding a fixed position. The burned angels screamed as they fell. Some were cut in half by the beam. A few lost wings, which fluttered toward the glowing streets of gold like rotten dry leaves that held on to their branches until the cold heart of winter. The beam persisted for a moment, and though Apollo aimed his hand carefully, none of the gods or goddesses understood why Apollo didn't redirect his aim toward Toliq, who'd only moved slightly to one side. She watched the white-hot laser next to her with a dull fascination, but she didn't move any farther from it.

The beam disappeared and Apollo lowered his arm.

"You missed," Inanna sneered.

"You're right, of course," Apollo said dryly. "I'm very sad about that."

Baldur didn't understand Apollo's strategy or his response, but he knew his friend was attempting some stratagem. "Well, if that didn't work, shall we to arms then?"

"It's time," Apollo agreed.

Baldur reached behind him into some other dimension and retrieved his voulge, a long pole with a cleaver for a head. The weapon gleamed like the sun itself, and when he spun it, the flash danced along the dark gray skin of the circling seraphim. Apollo made a similar gesture and revealed his bow, loading it from the quiver on his back with his famous poisoned arrows. These were the arrows of light that killed the sons of Niobe on contact. Now he pointed one at Inanna's face. His fingers slid from the string.

The arrow flew true, as always, but stopped just before the poisoned point touched her nose. The goddess gripped the fragile shaft in her hand for the briefest moment, then placed her thumb against the side and snapped it in half. She dropped the pieces toward the street below. "God of knowledge, you have underestimated my power." She, too, reached back and then revealed a gleaming knife with a long, curved blade. She held the knife up over her head and shouted, "Take them!"

The sphere contracted as the seraphim dived toward the gods at the core of the globe. Baldur swung the voulge in a wide arc, lopping off the first clawed hands that tried to grab him. Apollo aimed and fired three arrows. Seraphim screamed in brief agony, then turned to corpse-shaped missiles. Apollo and Baldur dodged these and made some space for themselves to work.

Baldur looked through the incoming cloud of dark gray leather for glimpses of Ekkeko, Horus, and Enlil, then began to carve his way toward them. Seraphim fell before him, limbs spinning away as the voulge helicoptered through the angry, scaled mass. But as the whirling polearm neared Horus, Baldur felt it strike metal and change direction. Horus deflected with his decorative sword, then punched Baldur with the hilt. As Baldur reeled, dozens of hands wrapped around his arms and legs. Claws pierced his clothing and the flesh beneath. While paralyzed, he felt the blade of Horus' sword pierce his side and exit through his liver. He knew the wound could not kill him. His mother's power protected him. Still, the wound hurt like a bitch.

Apollo didn't last much longer. The arrows in his quiver reappeared as quickly as he could send them flying, but he couldn't keep up with the onslaught. He felt a burst of hope when the seraphim seemed to hesitate. Perhaps, he speculated, mercenaries didn't like suicide missions. Then he saw Enlil, god of air and political discourse, weave at his unholy speed through the retreating crowd, and knew he couldn't compete. He loosed two arrows in Enlil's direction, but the god dodged them easily, twisting like a snake around the poisoned heads, letting the dove feather fletchings caress him as they passed. And then Enlil was upon him, striking as quickly and cruelly as an anonymous Internet message board. As he smashed his little fists into Apollo's face, Enlil belted-out a litany of technical political terminology as if he were casting a spell of staccato curses. "Socialist - fascist - terrorist - neo con - isolationist - utopian - bureaucrat - colonialist - multilateralist - special interest - racist - communist - exceptionalist - ideologue - Democrat - Republican - imperialist - conservative - corporatist - liberal!" The skin on Apollo's beautiful face split above his eye, in his nose, behind both lips, on his cheek. Blood covered Enlil's hands, but he continued. As Apollo fell backward, seraphim grabbed him and held him in place so Enlil could do more damage.

"Bring them to me," Inanna commanded. The space between the goddesses and the prisoners opened, and the seraphim dragged Apollo and Baldur toward Inanna while Ekkeko and Horus followed, smirking, and Enlil wiped the blood off his hands with a silk handkerchief. Apollo was too dazed to move, but Baldur, his wound already healed, continued to struggle.

"Toliq?" Inanna asked. "The mistletoe, please?"

Toliq pulled a small sprig of mistletoe out of her pocket, floated over Baldur's head, and held the leafy twig just above his forehead. Baldur looked up at it, knowing of its power.

"Your mother forgot to protect you from only one thing," Inanna said. "Figuring out what that was...no easy task. And once I knew, imagine how hard it was for me to just sit on that kind of secret. But as you saw in Paris, I can be patient." She floated in front of him, smiling, then moved toward him so fast it seemed she'd pounced. She clung to his chest, holding on to handfuls of his shirt, and kissed him hard. Her feet left the stirrups created by the hands of seraphim holding his thighs, sliding between the gray, scaled flesh until she locked her ankles and squeezed, grinding herself against his stomach as she kissed him. The hands of three seraphim gripped him by the hair so that he couldn't escape her kiss. Her teeth sank into his lower lip, first a gentle nibble, then growing pressure. He felt the flesh slowly distend like a boil, then burst. She leaned back, licking her lips, then dove in again, this time sticking out her tongue and carefully running a line of his own blood from the tip of his nose, up his forehead, to his hairline. Then she rolled her head back, still rubbing herself against him, and hummed a long, satisfied purr. She ran one hand up along his face, then grabbed a bit of exposed blond hair which wasn't gripped by a seraph. Her head snapped forward. She looked into his eyes. Then she hauled hard to one side, tilting his head despite the efforts of the seraphs who held it, causing them to rip some of his hair out. Now, with his neck exposed, she cried, "Do it!"

Toliq screamed, a high-pitched bark of vengeful glee, and stabbed the point of the tiny sprig of mistletoe down into Baldur's neck four times. The puncture wounds were very small. Droplets of blood appeared on the surface of his skin, but didn't trickle down. Still, he could feel his strength draining away. Frigga's spells of warding became a curse as this tiny, innocuous twig did its damage. Horus' blade had hurt, but this felt like some poison which caused an undeniable and immediate drowsiness. His power had left him, and the absence felt like instant exhaustion.

While Toliq admired her handiwork, Inanna lost interest and floated over to Apollo. "Oh, Apollo, if you could see yourself now," she said.

Apollo could imagine the split lips, the broken skin, the rising bruises, the shattered cheek and the shard of bone which had entered his right orbital cavity and pierced the white of his eye, turning the white a dark red and causing him to cry blood.

"You were so beautiful, god of music, poetry, and art. Oh, what a wreck Enlil has made of you." She gestured to Baldur without looking at him. "You're weaker than your friend, now." She ran a hand down his face, gently, as she had with Baldur. "Such a shame." Then she stuck the tip of her finger into his eye, daubing it like a paintbrush, and painted a line up the ridge of his broken nose and his bruised forehead to his hairline. "Oh well," she said.

"Oh well," Toliq mimicked, laughing.

Inanna looked up at Toliq, who still hovered above Baldur's head, and winked at her. What a stupid, sycophantic ditz, she thought of her newest lover. Then Inanna looked through the crowd of seraphim to Horus, Ekkeko, and Enlil. "Let's do it," she said.

The three gods nodded. They floated down toward the golden street below, but stopped part-way. They went to work, making hand gestures as though digging small holes on a beach somewhere, and chanting different incantations. Horus, in a booming bass, cried out in the earliest form of his native tongue from Upper Egypt. Enlil whispered in a Hittite dialect. Ekkeko abandoned his native Inca for a Phoenician precursor to Mycenean Greek. But all three included some heavily accented form of the name "Tartarus." When Apollo heard this, even through the haze of pain, he sighed and his head lolled.

Between the bricks of the golden street below, liquid seeped through, dark red and steaming, like burgundy lava or boiling blood. It formed a ring that stretched across the width of the street. Then the bricks slid into the ground, falling away and revealing the hole. When the light peered over the edge of the pit it revealed the walls, not smooth and artificial or rough and stone in the mouth of a cave, but soft, wrinkled, pink, and wet like a hungry throat.

"Cast them down," Inanna commanded.

The seraphim, carrying the two wounded gods, floated down toward the yawning pit in a frenzied ball of leather wings. When they passed Ekkeko, Enlil, and Horus, the three gods exchanged glances. They knew better than to get so close, and they smiled at their shared secret.

"Goodbye, Apollo. Goodbye, Baldur," Inanna said. Her voice was soft but not regretful. She was, after all, a fertility goddess, and the sound of a post-coital farewell after a one night stand was not new to her.

"Goodbye!" Toliq shouted. Her voice carried a mad glee that made Inanna roll her eyes.

Tartarus inhaled. The seraphim nearest the mouth of the pit lost their places in the formation and were sucked in, screaming. The sound an angel makes when it falls cannot be accurately compared to anything else in any universe.

The hands holding Baldur and Apollo released and were replaced by clawed feet, pushing them down so that their seraphim owners could gain some tiny advantage as they fled the sucking pit. More seraphim fell along with the gods, but while the angels screamed, Baldur and Apollo, listless, bleeding, exhausted, defeated, bit down on the last of their dignity and descended in silence.

While the escaping seraphim achieved safe distance, the mouth of Tartarus began to seal up. It was not a hole into the center of Asgard, after all, nor was it a channel to any underworld housing the human dead. Tartarus didn't lead anywhere. Taratarus was a god, though one so primordial it came from a time before human form, a creature from a time when beings were so vast and had so little definition they could be both deities and places. Tartarus was little more than a throat and a stomach, just an appetite and a consequence, an abyss and an oubliette.

Up until that moment, Toliq knew nothing of these earlier gods, these monsters of the chaos at the beginning of time. But the sight of Tartarus tugged at her, activating her hunger and lust enough to trigger her slight, primitive intellectual curiosity. She marveled at this primordial power and imagined a universe filled with such creatures, where nothing made sense and blind mystery would be the only thing to see. The vision made her eyes water and filled her mouth with saliva.

When Tartarus had gone back to its place outside the dimension Yahweh had built for Asgard, it left only a ring of rich, freshly turned dirt in the middle of a street of gold to mark its appearance. But another hole remained beneath the City of God. Apollo's laser had crossed under the city horizontally, and was so pinpoint thin in places that it would have been nearly impossible to discover unless backlit by some revolving sun. Since no stars orbited around the floating mountain of Asgard, Inanna and her cohort could not discover it. Apollo's blast of white-hot light had punched beneath the city so that, with the utmost care, he could carve a message in a looping, feminine, cursive script. Apollo's last gambit had worked. In a suburb on the opposite side of the City, outlined in smoking, black burn marks on the white marble wall of

Artemis' bedroom, a simple Greek code directed Apollo's twin to warn Jesus about the not-normal man in Paris.

20

When a new batch of commercials came on, beginning with one for a local chain of car tire dealers, Joe pushed one of the presets on the car radio and found some news. He leaned back in the driver's seat and listened. The international situation was desperate, as usual. On the domestic front, the status quo of permanent crisis was being expertly maintained. Neither of these revelations surprised Joe. Worse, they didn't even disappoint him much anymore.

The hard news anchor tossed to the wacky morning radio guy, who shared some analysis of the major TV networks cancellations of some of their fall shows. The networks had decided that their new reality programming, though not reaching the historic highs of shows like *Survivor* and *The Amazing Race*, still garnered enough eyeballs to make them more profitable than scripted television that required inconveniences like actors, sets, and writers. Instead, the networks had noted the success of reality shows about idiots in New Jersey and Beverly Hills, and decided to see if they could compete with tamer versions of stupid-beautiful-people-behaving-badly programing in prime time.

In sports news, a prominent athlete who'd been convicted of sexual assault would be returning to the field after his much disputed three-game suspension.

Another television pundit had been fired by his hyper-partisan network for saying something that violated party dogma, and had been promptly hired and given a raise by an opposing hyper-partisan television network.

The final story, which the DJ relayed with particular amusement, was about a man in Alabama who'd been caught and charged with "killing or disabling livestock" after he'd sexually assaulted a miniature horse. He'd received that charge because the state of Alabama had no law on the books prohibiting bestiality. The man had been caught because he'd dropped his wallet at the scene of the crime.

Joe was reaching forward to change the station again when he was cut off. A co-ed in a Chevy Prism zipped past him, doing more than 80, and even though she dodged an oncoming tractor by lunging into his lane, she was going so fast he didn't have to slow down. Joe grabbed the wheel with both hands and squeezed until his knuckles turned white. He did have time to catch a quick glimpse of three of her bumper stickers as she pulled ahead. "You're a naughty boy. Go to my room," one said. "Why go for the pink when you can go for the stink?" the next asked. The word pink was written in that color, and stink was written in steaming brown letters. The third said, "My perfect man is a nymphomaniac who owns a liquor store."

It took Joe a second to release the wheel after the surprise, so he was treated to the first two verses and chorus of a song about how California girls wear the least clothing, will freak in a jeep, and are so hot they'll melt your popsicle. Joe had a strange and inexplicable feeling that some of the light, beauty, art, and intelligence had vanished from the universe.

He turned the radio off.

Joe looked up at the sky above them as they made their way down the long, winding, two-lane back road, farm land stretching to the hills on both sides. It should have been beautiful. It had always seemed so in the past. Oregon skies fill with more than their fair share of clouds, but even these generally provide texture. That day the sky was flat, the iron gray giving nothing to the harvested fields, emptied of grass seed and hops. On the hillsides, rows of struts held up the grape vines that twisted, naked and fruitless, in the angry wind. Joe tried to remind himself that he was headed home, but that didn't make him feel much better.

"So, how do you think that went?" he asked.

Andrew "Drew" Becker, the office's newest hire, rode shotgun, his laptop bag propped between his ankles, the gold University of Oregon pin gleaming proudly on the shoulder strap. "Well, she was nice."

"Yeah, I thought so."

"But she was old."

"And?" Joe said, smiling.

Drew tried to cover. "I just mean, you know, she doesn't need to do the same kind of financial planning."

"True. How did you handle that?"

"Well, I wanted to up-sell her at first. My dad likes to say that some people have lotsa dollars, but no sense. She was the opposite. She wasn't going to buy a million dollars of life insurance."

"Right."

"So we sold her enough to bury herself, basically. So that's pretty disappointing."

Joe shook his head. "No, Drew, don't look at it that way. You did really well. I like your read on her. Lot of sense, but not a lot of dollars. But think of what she does have."

"What? An old house? Too many cats?"

"She told us she has four kids. They are all in their 50s. She has a whole mess of grandkids, and a ton of great-grandkids. She's a matriarch of a huge clan."

"Yeah?"

"Yeah," Joe said. "So, imagine if you'd tried to hard-sell her on a bunch of stuff she didn't need. And imagine she'd bought it. She can pay in on those policies for, what, 20 years?"

"If she's lucky."

"Right. But before she could do that, one of her kids would figure out she didn't need all that and cut those policies off. And your residuals would disappear. But you did really well, because you were very nice to her, but, better than that, you respected her intelligence. That was a good call. Older folks hate being treated like they're senile just because they're old. So you explained things clearly, but not in a condescending way. So she gets a little term life policy that's within her means and would pay for her funeral if she died before the term ended. If she pays it off she'll be able to renew, though the rates would be pretty high when she's in her 90s. And you were honest about that. And she appreciated that. So, maybe you didn't make much. But if she tells her kids about the great insurance salesman she met today, what will they think, right away?"

"They'll think I was probably some jerk salesman trying to take advantage of her."

"Right. And they'll run over to see how she got ripped off. And then they'll see that you didn't do that, and maybe you get a call. And maybe that kid passes your name on to two of his kids. And maybe one of them buys enough insurance to protect his young family in case he dies suddenly. Only, he won't because he's young and healthy. He's just smart enough to be protected because he got his grandma's genes. So you collect residuals on that larger policy for the rest of your life."

"Maybe," Drew said.

Joe frowned. "Well, maybe this sale and maybe the next, but there's no maybe about it in the long run. It's a numbers game. And this is what I like about insurance. We're rewarded not for ripping people off, but for giving them something that's actually valuable and smart. And we are rewarded more if we're honest and kind and professional. How many careers are like that?"

"Not many."

They rode in silence for a bit. Joe suspected Drew didn't really take him all that seriously. And why would he? Joe was just an old guy puffing up his own line of work and ranting about honesty and kindness. He wasn't a rock star. They were riding in a Nissan Maxima, after all. Joe was just a graduate from a small college, a manager at a small-town branch office, a man who'd barely had dreams to give up on. If he told the much younger man that he suspected his wife was fucking another guy, would Drew have been surprised by anything other than his candor?

Drew startled him when he asked, "So, do you still get residuals?"

"Some. But I took a big cut in the percentage of mine when I went into management. Now I get a cut of the whole office. That's to keep me from sitting around the office with my feet up on my desk. My job is making you successful. If you succeed, I succeed. That's why it's a good business. It rewards some greed, but it gets wrecked by too much greed. That goes all the way up the chain.

"You could have up-sold that old lady," Joe explained, "but you'd be screwing yourself in the long run. And I could have told you to, but I'd be screwing myself in the long run. And the CEO could tell me to, but he'd be guaranteeing himself a short tenure. And the stockholders could demand that he make massive quarterly profits, but they'd be screwing themselves in the long run. That's what happens to lots of firms. They get into the financial planning side too much, filling their annuities with sketchy hot stocks and all kinds of weird financial instruments."

"Like housing derivatives?"

"Exactly. And the CEO is happy. And the stockholders are happy. And then a bubble bursts, and the firm isn't properly capitalized, and everybody loses. That's why we're never going to be the hot stock. We're a boring old blue chip. Slow growth. We're in it for the long haul."

Joe stopped when he said that. An image had flashed in his mind, the sight of Christy turning and heading back down the hall, out to the car, off to who knows where. Joe was in it for the long haul. And he was a boring old blue chip. Was that what was driving her out the door?

"Are you hot in here?" Joe asked.

Drew shook his head. "I'm good."

Joe swallowed. "Sorry. I think I'm getting car sick."

"Oh man, Joe, put the air on. That's cool with me."

"No," Joe said, "I think I'd better pull over."

He slowed carefully, then pulled onto the gravel on the shoulder. Tall grass hid a steep dip into a run-off ditch, but Joe didn't sink the car into it. Once the car was parked, he looked in his rear-view mirror, made sure it was safe, and opened his door. He climbed out, walked around the front of the car, and stepped over the ravine into the grass. He bent and spit, but didn't really feel nauseous. He walked two steps further, between some tall bushes, and leaned his forearms on the wooden fence, careful not to touch the wire that ran along the inside.

"You okay?" Drew called.

"I just need a minute."

"Cool," Drew shouted.

As if in response, the buffalo lifted its head from the grass it had been cropping.

"Holy shit!" Joe hissed and stood up straight.

The massive bison stood only a few feet from the fence. Somehow Joe hadn't seen it, or had mistaken it for a giant pile of dirt or something. Joe looked down the road and saw the large, oval, wrought-iron sign swaying in the wind. "Dakota Heritage Ranch" it said around a flat iron cut-out of a buffalo. Looking up the steep hill, Joe saw a few other large brown mounds dotting the green and beige field, but all high up. The rest of the herd must have been over the hill, where the road wound to the farm itself, hidden somewhere far off. This lone bison was far from its family, standing down next to the road, minding its own business until some straight-out-of-U-of-O kid shouted "Cool," and startled him. Now he stared at Joe warily with one huge, black eye.

Joe marveled at the roundness of the bison's eye. Set beneath a short 'fro of brown curls and an almost-white horn pointing outward and then straight up in the air, and on a horizontal plane with a small, twitching ear, the black orb studied him carefully, measured him, then closed halfway as the huge head sank back to the grass. What had that eye seen? A predator? It should have, Joe knew. Once, thousands (perhaps millions, for all Joe knew) of this buffalo's ancestors had ruled the Great Plains. Then they'd been hunted nearly to extinction by men just like him. Then someone who also looked like Joe, probably with the best of intentions, had rounded up this guy's father or grandfather and had brought him to Oregon somehow. Joe looked down at the fence. Just moments ago it had been holding him up, keeping him from falling forward. Now his fingertips barely gripped it but it kept him from falling backward away from the creature who had startled him so much. Did the fence make the bison feel safe? Or trapped?

Joe thought about his own ancestors. His grandfather, surrounded by an electrified fence in a camp in Germany. Surely he'd felt trapped, just like the buffalo. And he must have known he was going to be slaughtered, too. So he'd worked for the guards. He'd betrayed God's chosen people. Desperate. Joe could understand, in a way, though he couldn't forgive. He could never forgive his grandfather because the curse was all his fault. Down to the fourth generation. Grandfather, father,

Joe himself, then Dawkins. Dawkins would have to meet with Yahweh for coffee just like he did. Joe would tell Dawkins not to fight it, but Dawkins would. After all, Joe had. He'd tried to refuse to show up, but he'd just wake up on that barstool in Andy's. He'd tried to tell Christy, but she'd just looked at him blankly, unable to hear what she was not allowed to know. It was a curse, after all. The perfect curse for the Jewish atheist Freudian psychiatrist turned prison snitch in a Nazi concentration camp: to have to listen to God Himself complain and not be able to tell anyone, not be able to publish the greatest case study in human history. But how did that fit an insurance salesman in Independence, Oregon 60 years later? And how did it fit Dawkins, his perfect, funny, loving son who didn't know anything about Jews or Nazis or Hebrews and their God but just wanted to read his Chronicles of Narnia and believe in Aslan? Why subject him to a curse designed for his great-grandfather? Dawkins would come to hate his great-grandfather. He'd probably blame Joe, too, but Joe knew he'd figure out that he couldn't have been warned. Would that be enough for his son to forgive him? Probably, on some rational level. But a forgiveness that reached down to some deeper place where our resentment lives and makes us hate people without even knowing why? Joe worried even Dawkins' forgiveness wouldn't reach that far. Especially not once he learned that the God of mercy held grudges for four generations. Why should he forgive?

Joe looked at the way the bison's back rose to a high point above his shoulders. Even on all fours, the animal looked like it was standing proudly, the way a man might throw his shoulders back and stick out his chest to have a medal pinned on it. The buffalo didn't look upward like some proud douchebag being honored at a medal ceremony, or, worse, like those athletes who look up at the sky and point in mock-humility, gesturing, "The credit for this touchdown, for my athletic prowess and its most recent manifestation on the field, belongs not to me but to Jesus who has chosen this humble vessel over the less blessed team I just scored on." Joe didn't mind pride. He liked the receivers who gave a flying chest bump to the guys who blocked for them, then inclined their heads forward and pointed back at the quarterbacks who made the passes and the linemen who protected them. That was the proper mixture of pride and humility, in Joe's opinion. The buffalo had that, only it wasn't pride in his team, but a pride in his species built into his genetic make-up. His high back and face on the ground said, "I don't need to brag or look up at the sky and thank Jesus for making me a buffalo. I'm just a buffalo. But I am a buffalo. Two thousand pounds of bone and muscle that can come at you at 35 miles per hour. So show some fucking respect."

Joe thought about the buffalo's nobility. It would have every right to be ashamed. Its species had ruled the plains. Now they foraged between larger fields of hops and grass seed, watching their future. Someday a yuppie would play a game of golf on the grass grown from that seed, drink a microbrew made from those hops, and eat an over-priced, lean, guilt-absolving burger made from this guy's ass. So what did the buffalo have to be proud about? He was a remnant of a species that had passed its prime, living a constrained life and doomed to an embarrassing and trivial end. He was just a buffalo. But he was a buffalo. And worthy of some respect.

Joe's chest swelled. He was the weaker son of a stronger father, but he was not a weak man. He was just an insurance salesman, but he was honest and kind and a teacher and leader. Sure, his work only made the world better in a tiny way. Grandma back there would sleep easier at night, and she wouldn't leave her kids a $10,000 funeral bill when she kicked it. It was small, but it was something good. More important, he could raise a strong, bright boy who would grow to be his better. And he was a faithful and supportive husband. No, more than that. He chose to love his wife even if she might be unfaithful. That was up to him and he chose to love her. His grandfather's treachery and his own ignominious nursing-home death be damned. Yahweh, "Manny," with his complaining and his disdain for human concerns: damn Him, too. Because Joe chose to love his wife even when it was difficult, maybe even pointless, and that might not be something to brag about, might not be something to stick your chin out about or look up and give credit to Jesus about, but it was something to be proud of when your face was on the dirty ground. So show some fucking respect!

Joe nodded to the bison. It didn't respond, but Joe didn't need it to. It was his comparison, not a transcendental sign from the universe. If anything, it was better that the buffalo went on cropping the grass. Joe decided that was about right. He stepped back over the drainage ditch, through the high grass, and walked around the car on the gravel shoulder.

"Feeling better?" Drew asked.

Joe climbed into his seat. "Yeah, I just needed some air. There was a buffalo over there. Startled me a little."

Drew turned and tried to see it through the tall grass and bushes along the fence. "Really? Cool! They're pretty amazing, huh?"

Joe started the car. "Yeah, they're…." He struggled to find the word.

"Quietly noble," Drew said.

Joe decided he'd underestimated his new hire.

21

Ghair Aadi closed the laptop with a sense of triumph. It was done. The video was sent. The decoded clip would be burned onto a CD in Doha, Qatar's capital, and delivered to a reporter in exactly four days. By then, people would be wondering about the strange illness that was popping up in major cities around the world, but they wouldn't realize it was a full biological attack quite yet. Once they did, and once some computer experts from the NSA and Interpol had the Al Jazeera video to work with, they'd crack the code and trace the transmission back to this apartment. By then, it would be far too late. Sure, they'd round up his roommates, who would be sent off to CIA black sites and tortured, but because they knew so little of his work they'd only confirm the lie of the tape: that al Qaeda was responsible, and that the attacker was Iranian.

While the sickness spread, the forces of the West would mobilize on his homeland. They would say they were fighting for justice, or to depose the mullahs. They would demand that Iran turn over its nuclear arsenal, and since it didn't have one yet, they'd probably invade. With any luck, Ghair Aadi's video would unite the fringe Sunni who supported al Qaeda with the most die-hard Shia of the Iranian hardliners. The enemy of my enemy is my friend, after all. Who knew how far the destabilization would go in the name of religion? If China cracked down harder on its Muslim population at the behest of the West (since they were just looking for an excuse to do so, anyway), would they find themselves in another conflict with Pakistan? Would the moderates in Indonesia, the world's fourth-largest country, be activated by the holy war? Certainly someone would blame the infection on the Israelis, as some kind of double-cross plot to implicate Islam for their own benefit. It hadn't taken long for someone to do so after 9/11. You could always count on somebody out there to blame the Jews, and some other fool to believe it.

You are going to change the world, one of the voices in his head said.

You know that Chinese proverb about how the symbol for difficult times is opportunity? the other voice asked. Well, this is going to cause a whole lot of that symbol.

Ghair Aadi generally felt like he could tell what the second voice was trying to say, but he couldn't figure out how she so frequently managed to avoid saying it clearly or correctly. Plus, he knew this factoid was just an urban legend used by

American CEOs and politicians. How could his own hallucination be so dumb?

Right, um, well, said the first voice, it's time to get this done.

I just think it's time to man-up there, the second voice said.

Ghair Aadi conceded that it took a certain amount of courage to inject one's self with a genetically modified super-virus, but he felt that "man-up" was the wrong advice. After all, he was a self-aware schizophrenic who was both suicidal and genocidal. It wasn't really a question of testosterone, but of pure, conscious madness. He knew it wasn't sociopathy; he was capable of feeling remorse. Just not for this. He could feel embarrassment when he made some social faux pas. He could remember deep shame when scolded by his mother at age 13 when she caught him looking in a department store catalogue at the models, some of whom modeled frumpy, utilitarian underwear. But that was before the voices, before he'd made a choice to reject conventional morality and go out with a bang. Or at least a flourish.

He took a syringe and drove the needle into the rubber stopper on one of the glass vials standing on his desk. Then he drew the solution out of the vial, carefully watching the yellowish liquid rise to a specific height in the syringe. He yanked up the short sleeve of his shirt over his shoulder and stuck the needle into the meat of his arm, then depressed the stopper. It hurt a bit, the pain traveling down his arm to his thumb, but the sting subsided quickly. Then he took the six vials, all standing together in their plastic holder, and dropped them into his simple office trash can, which he'd lined with a plastic grocery bag. He'd have to throw them away outside the airport so they'd be disposed of before anyone could search his apartment/laboratory and use the original virus to search for a cure. He tossed the used microscope slides in as well, then the Petri dishes. He looked at the desk for a moment, thought about it, and swept all the remaining tools into the trash, where he had to stomp on them to get the broken glass to fit. He'd already cleaned up the dead mice and the equipment that kept their cages ventilated but separated from the external air. That had been a more careful job, back when he'd had to be careful not to get infected too soon. Now, it didn't matter. He was just hiding evidence. The infection had already begun.

He made a quick call to the cab company, took his small, rolling suitcase and set it by the door, and came back into his office. He carefully put his computer into his carry-on bag, then tossed the glass in the small trashcan into a larger kitchen trash bag. As he waited for the cab, he sat down at the kitchen table and scribbled a note on the pad of paper the roommates used to leave one another phone messages.

"My brothers, I have been called upon to leave Paris for a mission. Of course I cannot share the details, but I do not expect to return to Paris, so I have left you a month's rent and my food in the refrigerator. May Allah bless you all and keep you from harm." Ghair Aadi laughed aloud at his joke. The milk in the fridge was expired. The check for rent would bounce. And it didn't matter. He knew they would all be sick or in CIA custody in four days.

The cabbie on the street honked his horn, two short, sharp blasts. Ghair Aadi picked up his rolling bag, his carry-on, and the white trash-bag, and he walked out the door.

He stepped out the front door onto the sidewalk of the Rue de Steinkerque, and was greeted by a friendly-looking man with a dark, curly beard and a baseball cap that advertised for the Chicago Cubs. The poor, immigrant cab driver also wore a t-shirt with the name of some American rock band he'd probably never heard of. Ghair Aadi guessed the man was a Muslim, and the thought made him snort a little laugh. He thought this somehow fitting for his mission to destroy any belief in God; first some jihadists (including himself, the world's first atheist Arab extremist), then a poor Muslim immigrant, then a million Parisians, Londoners, New Yorkers, and on through America before another hop to Tokyo, then Hong Kong, Shanghai, Moscow, and back to Europe, where he'd probably be too sick to get on another flight. Would he make it to Berlin or Athens or Rome? He'd only bought tickets through Madrid. He looked away from the cab driver, down the street, then up to the Basilica at the top of the hill. He was glad to be rid of this city, at least.

"*Puis-je prendre vos bagages?*" the man asked in heavily accented French.

Before Ghair Aadi could say, "*Oui,*" the man had grabbed the handles of both bags and pulled them from his hands. Once they were in the little car's trunk, the cabbie came back for the garbage bag.

"*Est cette poubelle?*" the cabbie asked.

Again, before Ghair Aadi could tell the man it was garbage (or lie and claim it was dirty clothes that only sounded like broken glass), the man took it. He twisted the bag so that it inflated like a balloon, then thought better of it, released it so that it spun, and let the air inside blow out. Then, while leaning it on his leg to release more of the air, he twisted it again, producing a smaller balloon. As he did this, he joked, "*Il ne pue pas!*"

Ghair Aadi couldn't help but laugh, and agreed that the contents of the bag didn't stink. In fact, he'd worked quite hard to make them odorless. Just when he thought the man couldn't do any more to infect himself, when the cabbie returned from the trunk he put out his hand and shook Ghair Aadi's with that kind of vigor reserved for eager immigrants.

"*L'aéroport, je suppose?*" the cabbie said, releasing his hand.

Ghair Aadi said, "*Oui,*" and climbed into the back of the cab.

Before the cab driver got behind the wheel he put a finger to one side of his nose, inhaled sharply, and shot a gob of snot on the sidewalk directly in front of the door to the apartment. Ghair Aadi felt a flash of irritation, and wondered if the man was trying to insult him, then remembered he would never be returning and decided to be amused by such an uncouth and plebian act.

As they made their way to Charles de Gaulle, the cab driver shoved in a cassette tape (something Ghair Aadi hadn't seen in so long it was a bit of a curiosity) and pressed play. The beginning of the song, just the first few bars, was a particularly mournful tune played on an electric guitar. Then the drums kicked in and the sound of Jimi Hendrix singing "Red House" mixed with the voice of the cab driver, who ignored the words and hummed along with the guitar which danced around the simple blues melody in an incredibly complex, virtuoso performance. The cab driver mimicked it almost perfectly, only a couple of times he slipped into an ululation that harmonized, and when he did this he'd look back at Ghair Aadi in the rear view mirror and wink. Ghair Aadi presumed the man must have only a few cassettes, perhaps only this one, and had listened to it thousands of times to memorize such a complex part. He wondered if the man understood English, and knew what the song was about. It was simple story of a man who hasn't visited his girlfriend in "99 and one half days", returns to her red house to find that his key won't get him in, and decides to go back the way he came and replace the woman with her sister. The song was either a kind of paraprosdokian joke, or a bit of disgusting chauvinism, or both, but the lyrics were clearly not the point. Still, Ghair Aadi thought the man should at least know what he was singing along with.

Forget about the cab driver, the first voice said.

Yeah, said the second. You're kinda losing focus there a teensy bit.

"Sorry," Ghair Aadi said.

"*Quoi?*" asked the cabbie.

"*Rien,*" Ghair Aadi said. "*Pardon.*"

The cabbie smiled, nodded, and went back to his strange singing.

By happenstance, when they pulled up to the curb at de Gaulle, the driver parked right next to a trashcan. He got out, popped the trunk, and set Ghair Aadi's carry-on and rolling bag carefully on the sidewalk. Then, as Ghair Aadi stood by his bags, the cabbie handed him the white plastic trash bag.

"*Avez un bon voyage,*" the man said.

Ghair Aadi stood by his bags for a moment, watching the cab go. The man had been so friendly he couldn't bring himself to throw the bag away until the taxi had passed out of sight. The irony of this was not lost on Ghair Aadi. He knew he'd just killed the man, but he refused to insult him in the process. Once the cab had curved away, he tossed the bag in the trashcan and picked up his luggage.

As he passed through security, he thought about this strange discontinuity. Was his video a similar insult? Why lie to the people he was killing? Was starting a holy war only adding insult to injury? The virus would do enough to vent his hatred toward the universe that had stricken his brilliant mind with schizophrenia. Why compound this lashing out with some pedantic attempt to destroy the illusion of God with a horrific war in the midst of his plague?

Don't lose your resolve now, the first voice said.

You've got to keep your eye on the ball, the second said.

"I don't have to do anything," he said as he walked down the terminal toward his gate. "That's the point. It's all pointless."

And isn't a holy war fought over a non-existent God the ultimate expression of the pointlessness of existence? the first voice asked. The virus is just a means to cause that war. The war is the real rebellion against your plight.

"You are my plight. You are my curse. I could have just killed myself."

We're too big for that. Your suffering is too great, dontcha think? asked the second. Finish the doing of what you gotta do, and you won't just be dead. You'll be vindicated.

Ghair Aadi frowned. "We'll see."

22

Joe sat in the chair in Dawkins' room, reading Prince Caspian while Dawkins fell asleep.

"...was like meeting very old friends. If you had been there you would have heard them saying things like, 'Oh, look! Our coronation rings —do you remember first wearing this? —Why, this is the little brooch we all thought was lost. —I say, isn't that the armor you wore in the tournament on the Lone Islands? —do you remember the dwarf making that for me? —do you remember drinking out of that horn? —do you remember, do you remember?'"

Joe looked up from the paperback. Silently, Christy had slipped into the room. He'd only felt her presence. She stood above him, looking down at their son. She turned to him when she noticed he'd stopped reading, then looked back at Dawkins and made a hand motion, a sideways karate chop that said the boy was not just asleep, but completely out. Joe picked up the bookmark, flipped back a page to make up for the story Dawkins had missed, and set the bookmark inside. He laid the book on Dawkins' dresser and followed Christy out of the room.

At the top of the stairs, he watched her descending. Did she want him to follow? he wondered. Or should he slip down the hall and lie down in his own bed with his own book. He knew he'd be avoiding her, and the thought pained him, but his anxiety about a real conversation, or, worse, a fake conversation, made him want to hide out upstairs.

As Christy turned down the hall, she brushed against Frigga, who leaned, unseen, against the front door. Joe walked down the stairs and passed the goddess. Frigga could have read so much from Joe's pace, his heavy steps, his tense shoulders, his head slightly bowed. She might have identified the nature of the conversation in that posture. But she didn't. She knew what they would say to one another, knew how the conversation would go, but she wanted to understand it in the moment, the way her husband could. She thought this might give her some insight into Yahweh's mind. She thought she might learn something about her son, Thor. His fixation on courage was a mystery to her, as well. Either the battle would be won or lost, and she knew which, so why did he leap into battle to test himself? She thought this conversation might teach her something about her step-son Jesus, too. She knew she loved Yahweh because she would love him, and will love him, and would have loved him in the future. But Jesus loved everyone in the present, regardless of their future and past. How did this work? Maybe this moment could teach her something. Of course, she'd come because she knew it would teach her. She even knew what she would learn, yet had to learn it anyway. She didn't question this. It was her gift and curse.

Joe stepped into the kitchen and thought about getting something to drink. He stood in front of the fridge, considering the bottles of beer and cans of soda behind the door, and the water dispenser in it.

"Come sit next to me," Christy said. She was on the couch, sitting sideways, arranging a blanket over her legs.

He nodded and postponed the beverage, knowing he might need a reason to get up soon. He sat down next to her, facing the TV. She flapped the blanket, an extra-long polar fleece, over his legs, then slid her feet across his lap.

"Wanna see what's on TV?" he asked.

"No," she said.

Okay, he thought. So we're doing this. "Okay," he said aloud, but more carefully, intentionally devoid of any meaning.

Frigga now stood behind the couch. She frowned. How they struggled, not knowing what to say. They'd each prepared so many lines, their quivers full of deadly arrows, but they would use so few, and she knew every one. How it hurt them not to know which.

"I need to tell you something," Christy said.

"Okay," Joe said, too quickly. "But only if you want to. You don't have to for me."

Christy looked down. "I know. But I have to. Because I don't think it's what you think."

She waited. Joe didn't speak. Christy wasn't sure if she was glad for his silence, or if a guessing game would have been a relief. After all, if she could have alleviated his worry, if she could know….

Frigga saw this on Christy's face. If the wife could know that the man suspected the worst, she could comfort him with her news. It would be bad, but less bad. In that case, she'd want him to accuse her. But if his guess was something else, her comfort could become a horrible revelation. And she couldn't know. Frigga saw this. She couldn't know.

"I think I…." Christy tried. "I worry you think I—I know I have not been …present."

"Yeah?"

"And I'm worried you think I've been, you know…."

"Have you?"

"Have I what?"

"I don't know," Joe said. "What have you been?"

"I haven't been unfaithful," Christy said.

Joe breathed hard out of his nose, then looked down at the floor. "Okay."

"But…."

"But?"

Christy flinched. "No, I mean…." She swallowed. "I haven't cheated on you. I haven't."

"But?"

"But I thought about it."

Joe looked at her. "Like, daydream thought about it or making plans thought about it?"

"Neither."

Joe raised one eyebrow.

Christy pressed the palm of her hand against her forehead. "Somewhere in between?"

"You don't have to tell me," Joe said.

"But I want to explain."

Joe's jaw clenched. She could feel his stomach tighten with the side of her leg. His anger tightened his lips. "Why?" he asked.

"Why?"

"Why do you want to explain?"

"So you know why I didn't do it, and that I won't do it."

Joe closed his eyes and leaned his head back, then stretched his neck muscles by rolling it slowly in a circle. He tried to take a deep breath, but took three short ones instead. "Okay."

"Okay?"

"Okay, I'm listening."

Christy nodded. "Do you remember that night?"

"When you took off? In the rain? In the dark? Crying? And Dawkins asked what was wrong and I had to lie and say you were fine but I couldn't make anything up fast enough and he knew I was lying? That night? Yes, I remember."

He hadn't raised his voice at all, but she was crying now. Frigga knew she'd cry, but now she knew why. The wife was just now realizing how she'd hurt her husband. Not by cheating, or thinking about cheating. By not telling him. Because he didn't already know. Frigga saw this in a new way. The not knowing: that was the cutting weapon. But the wife hadn't known to tell him. Or to lie. She'd known she would hurt him, but she hadn't known how. Frigga marveled.

"I wasn't going to cheat," Christy said. "I didn't know where I was going. I just saw you two, and felt so guilty for even thinking about hurting you, and I just couldn't take it, and I went and got in the car. And I didn't know where I was even going, but I went to his apartment."

She paused, waiting for Joe to ask whose apartment. He didn't.

"And then I went in and told him I would never cheat on you, even though he'd never asked or hit on me or done anything inappropriate. I just ambushed him with it, like a crazy person."

"And? What did he say?"

"He said it would be too strange to ever see me again. So he's moving away."

Joe looked at her. A tiny bit of a smile twisted the edge of his clenched lips. "Really?"

Christy smiled. "Yep."

"You scared him into moving out of town?"

"Out of state. Across the country."

Joe chuckled. Just once. Christy laughed too, and her face flushed. Then Joe let himself laugh some more. The last few days, the tiptoeing, the elliptical orbits, the magnetic barrier of avoided conversation: it all burst, and he let himself laugh. He put his big hands on her knee and ankle and held on while he pitched forward and laughed. Every laugh wanted to start with a hard consonant, like little coughs, like they wanted to escape and he couldn't hold them in.

"You are…." he tried, but couldn't continue. "You…."

"What?" she said, scolding but smiling.

"You really are a crazy person!" Now there were tears in his eyes. "You're some homeless lady on a bus walking up to the driver and saying, 'I will not cheat on my husband with you. So there!'"

Some tiny part of Christy's ego reminded her that Luke had felt it, too. He would have, if she'd wanted to. She was sure of it. But, she reminded herself, the homeless lady on the bus might find that the driver wants her, too, and is disappointed by her announcement. It doesn't make her any less crazy. This thought, this image of a disappointed bus driver, this simple narrative of the strange exchange of mutual unexpected rejection flashed through her mind. And then the woman got off the bus and the driver took off for New York with a bus full of screaming, trapped passengers. At this thought, Christy really lost it, and soon she was laughing even harder than Joe.

Frigga watched this laughter. For those millennia, when she'd been married to Odin, she was the only other immortal allowed to sit on his high thrown, Hliðskjálf, the seat from which one could see the whole universe. She'd sat there watching it all, silent, knowing the future of all Yahweh's creation, and this laughter had always vexed her. Sure, she could mimic the sound, but she could never feel amusement. It required the ability to be surprised. At times she'd wished she could hate them for it, all the gods who refrained from knowing so they could be startled into laughter, all the braying, stupid mortals shocked into their guffaws by a universe they couldn't comprehend, a universe they foolishly expected to behave in a certain way which always behaved in a different one. Why would they laugh, when their ignorance was equal in scope to her knowledge? Shouldn't it have all been just as predictably surprising for them as it was known to her? And yet they laughed. And she could not hate them. She could only envy them.

She knew what she would do. She'd known before she came, of course. She would go against her nature. She would tell her husband the future, and he would change it. And then she would not know it anymore. The chain of events would break. And what would she be then? Would he see her as a diminished thing, and leave her? Would she end up in the retirement home with her one-eyed ex-husband? She didn't know. The choice to tell the future created a veil that hid it from her sight.

"Hey," Christy said.

"Yeah?"

Frigga cringed at the pun before it was spoken.

"I'm still crazy about you."

Joe groaned. "Har har."

Christy placed her hand on Joe's. "But I want to tell you something else."

"Okay," he said. He didn't sound as worried this time.

"When I came in that night and saw you reading to Dawkins, I didn't leave because of him. It wasn't one of those 'staying together for the kids' things. It was you. And I want you to know that. I love you, in part, because of the father you are, but that doesn't mean I love you because of Dawkins. I love you more than I did the day we got married, but I'm not with you because of him. Does that make sense?"

He took his hand off her ankle and placed it on hers, so it was sandwiched between his and all three rested on her knee. "Yes. It does."

"I love you," she said.

"I love you. I would have loved you even if you'd cheated. I thought a lot about that, and I decided that I get to choose to love you, and nothing you can do can stop me." He smiled. "I love you even though you're a crazy person."

"But more as a crazy person than a cheater, right?"

"Well, yeah."

She pulled her hand out of his and placed hers against the side of his face. "I'm sorry," she said.

"I know. It's okay. And I'm sorry, too."

"Why?"

"Because I can't tell you that I'm cursed to have coffee with God every week, and that Dawkins is cursed, too," he said. He was surprised by how flat his voice sounded.

Of course, she couldn't hear him. "What?"

"I said I'm sorry I haven't been open enough about what's going on with me. I've been emotionally unavailable. And that probably…."

"No, this is all my fault."

"Well—"

"No. No, it's all my fault. And I'm sorry."

"Okay," he said. But Frigga knew he blamed himself. She also knew Christy was right. It wasn't Joe's fault he couldn't tell her about Yahweh. That was her husband's fault. She didn't know how that would turn out. It was on the other side of the veil. But she decided that, if she was going to give up on her gift, on herself, maybe on her marriage, she could at least try to do something for these two mortals. She'd given gifts before, but she'd always known their consequences and how they'd be received. For the first time, she felt that human sensation, giving a gift and wondering if it would be appreciated, if it would make a difference. Frigga felt her first sliver of hope.

She left the couple there on the couch and walked like a human for a few steps across their living room. She thought about her confession to her husband, sharing a glimpse of the future, lobbying for these people, breaking her nature, her self. She didn't know how it would turn out, but she wanted to do it anyway. Wrapped in fear and hope, she understood Thor just a bit better. If she could do it, this was courage. Of course, she would do it. This much she knew. But when she gazed into the future, courage was the end of her knowledge.

As she ascended toward Asgard, she knew this would make her son very proud.

23

The angel beneath them kept screaming as they fell.

"How long will he keep doing that?" Baldur asked Apollo.

"I don't know. Too long."

The walls of Tartarus, inky black in their depths, turned out to be made of pinkish flesh revealed by the light that shone out of the two glowing gods. Apollo and Baldur fell and fell through the esophagus that formed the primordial deity of the appetite of emptiness. Despite their divine powers, the two gods could not orient themselves properly, and they twisted and rolled like astronauts flailing in zero gravity. Also, they were separated by enough distance that they had to shout as they fell, which made conversation uncomfortable.

"Well, how long has he been screaming for now?" Baldur asked.

"Too long. Time has little meaning here. He could go on forever."

"Well, I wish he'd quit it."

Apollo shrugged as he spun. "He's a falling angel. What do you expect?" He sounded angry.

"Sorry," Baldur said.

"No, just, let's not try to talk for a while," Apollo said.

They stopped shouting and listened to the angel's screams for an indeterminate amount of time.

"Hey, I'm sorry," Apollo said.

"It's okay," Baldur called back. "Forsooth, this is an upsetting situation."

"It's more than that."

"What dost thou mean?"

"Look, Baldur, I may not be all-knowing like your mother, but I am a god of knowledge. I know a thing or two."

"Yeah?"

"Well, the word on the street is that if you are ever stabbed with mistletoe, you'll go down to the underworld."

Baldur looked around. "Check."

"And," Apollo explained, "Thor will try to get you back, but he won't be able to. You will be stuck in the underworld until Ragnarok, the final battle at the end of the universe."

"Oh."

"Yeah."

They listened to the seraphim's screams for a little while.

"So," Apollo continued, "you can imagine that I'm not too pleased to be with you right now."

"Maybe Thor can't save me, but maybe he can save you. Or maybe Artemis will come for you," Baldur theorized.

"Maybe."

"Don't give up hope, friend," Baldur called.

"Hope isn't a Greek virtue," Apollo yelled back. "It's an evil. False expectation is one of the curses Zeus tried to unleash upon the world as punishment for the trickery of Prometheus."

"Oh."

More silence from the gods. More screaming from the falling angel.

Then, there was a rumbling far beneath them.

"What was that?" Baldur shouted.

"I don't know!"

Because of the darkness, they had no warning. The walls of the tunnel contracted below them, closing like a tightened sphincter, and they slammed into the soft flesh of the new bottom of the pit. The sound of the seraphim disappeared as it was cut off from them.

Despite the soft flesh, the impact was considerable, and, combined with the shock, it took the gods a moment to stand up. Apollo walked over, taking ginger steps on the soft ground, and helped Baldur to his feet.

"We've stopped," Baldur said.

Apollo didn't feel an answer was required, so he stood still and looked upward into the darkness. With his divine eyesight, he thought he could see a tiny pinprick of light, smaller than a star, in the distance.

"See anything?" Baldur asked.

"Yes. I think we should get ready to run."

"What?"

There was another rumble.

"Run!" Apollo shouted. He grabbed the shoulder of Baldur's shirt and pulled the god behind him, running directly across the cylindrical bottom of the well toward the pink wall. Baldur had a brief moment of realization when the ground moved beneath his feet, passing backward toward the center of the new surface, and then both gods were launched upwards by a great, convulsive gag. Baldur didn't know what to do with his limbs, and he just flailed, but Apollo continued to run, his legs pin-wheeling in midair, and the floor reappeared beneath them a moment later, now much higher. Apollo pulled Baldur a bit closer to the wall, but just as they reached it, there was another convulsion and they were airborne again and moving ever higher. Then the floor beneath them yawned open, just as it had on the surface, only this time, instead of a gasping, sucking force pulling them down, a giant exhalation of air pushed them up the way they'd come with even greater force, and at a much greater speed.

Apollo looked up, aiming himself like a skydiver in reverse, watching the point of light in the distance. As they flew, the light grew, though it still seemed a distant speck until they were very close to it. Then, suddenly, it broadened to the width of Tartarus, and they were vomited back into the light.

Both gods flew into the air, high over the ground, and as they spun, trying to reorient themselves, they saw the golden streets of the City of God beneath them and, farther off, the horizon of the island of Asgard itself. Then their ascent hit its apex, and they started to fall, only much more slowly and under their own power.

"What happened?" Baldur asked.

"I don't know."

"Verily, it felt like we just got puked up."

Apollo frowned. "Well, yeah, but why?"

Baldur pointed down. "Let's ask them."

Below, the gods could just make out two tiny figures hovering above the mouth of Tartarus. As they descended, Tartarus closed up, and the people looked up to find them in the sky.

Baldur recognized his mother and step-father. "It's Frigga and Yahweh," he told Apollo.

Apollo sighed. "Let's see what they want."

They floated down to the CEO of the gods and his wife.

"Apollo, Baldur, there isn't much time," Yahweh said. "You need to go help Jesus. He's coming back to Asgard now, and Inanna and Toliq are waiting for him."

Baldur looked at his mother. "Is this Ragnarok?" Then to Yahweh. "Or the Apocalypse? The battle at the end of the universe?"

"I don't know," Frigga said. Then she did something he'd never seen. She laughed. It was a tiny laugh, and a bit of a sad one, but a laugh none-the-less. "It might be. Maybe I've done all this for nothing."

Yahweh put a heavy hand on Baldur's shoulder. "Your mother has chosen to speak of the future and change it. It's taken away her ability to see the future. She did this for you, Baldur." Yahweh knew this was a bit of an oversimplification. She'd done it for him, and for Jesus, and for Joe and Dawkins and Christy, and for herself, so she would gain the ability to laugh. But she'd also done it for Yahweh, though she wasn't quite sure why. Yahweh certainly didn't think He deserved it. But what was the point in telling Baldur all this? "So don't let her sacrifice be in vain." He pointed toward the edge of Asgard where Frigga had said Jesus would arrive. "Go. Now!"

24

When Jesus floated out of the void into the space just beyond the lip of the floating mountain of Asgard, he saw his wife at the outskirts of his father's city, and his first impulse was a very human one. He cringed. Muscles in his back, neck, colon, and face tightened. He didn't want to see her. He couldn't help it. He loved his wife. Sure, Jesus loved everyone, but loving Inanna was the most difficult love for him, because she had betrayed him so thoroughly. It wasn't just that she'd slept around. She had been a fertility goddess, and though he'd hoped, early in their marriage, that she would remain faithful, he'd grown to accept that some part of her could not escape from this aspect of her nature. Nor was it her lust for power, which was really just an extension of her libido. Sex, despite all efforts toward the egalitarian, is a ritual of negotiation, among other things. If she was a goddess of sex, all the aspects of the act itself were magnified within her to their logical conclusions. She lusted for pleasure, for sensation, for comfort, for connection, for affirmation, for submission, and, of course, for power. But while others participated in sex, she was all these lusts incarnate, and could not be satisfied. Because he loved her, he could forgive her for the most damaging manifestations of her tastes. After all, how could he hold a grudge against her for being the goddess he loved?

But he found it much harder to forgive her transgressions as the goddess of his church. He'd given her dominion over his institutional self, both as a symbol of his commitment to their matrimony and also as a means for her to be purified. He'd hoped she'd be able to channel her lusts into new forms as his perfect bride, lust for justice, lust for acceptance, lust for forgiveness, lust for peace, lust for devotion to himself and to his father. And she had failed. Even this he could have forgiven. After all, no god is perfect. Certainly she would err, and her church would occasionally go astray. He'd known that in advance, and had accepted it. It was a human institution, and would be prone to all human foibles.

Only Inanna had failed so spectacularly, and so intentionally, in her calling. She'd twisted his church quickly to her own aims. Perhaps, Jesus realized some fifteen hundred years ago, she'd entered into their marriage with the same ulterior motives he had. While he'd chosen a goddess who had already tapped into the well of human religion, and had hoped to turn her into something for his own sake, maybe she'd recognized him as a means to tap into some other vein she could not satisfy, a different kind of love than her Baalite adherents had mastered, and she had always hoped to use him in this way. Or perhaps it had been less intentional at first. He couldn't say. But regardless of her initial intentions, she'd quickly turned the church into a means to power, to wealth, to war, and to oppression. Even its emphasis on chastity, something she abhorred, had become a tool for her church to spurn people, alienate them from themselves and others, hate them, kill them. That was perhaps her greatest triumph: to use the church's focus on sexual purity as a means to fuck people over.

Jesus had lost the war before he became aware of the first battle. One day the Roman Empire was killing his saints, feeding them to lions for proclaiming his divinity, and Jesus' focus was on expanding his church so that all his father's people could learn to love one another. His first step, a humble and reasonable goal, was to stop them from feeding each other to lions. And then Inanna made it happen. And Jesus was pleased.

He didn't know how she'd done it. He didn't know that she'd begun to cheat with Horus, the god of kings and politicians, and Horus, in turn, had manipulated Constantine into negotiating a compromise with the Christians. The deal was simple. He'd stop killing them and accept them into mainstream Roman society on the condition that they renounce pacifism. After all, their continued growth in numbers was a threat to his rule, but converting to a pacifist faith would have been a disaster for a military general who maintained order through force of arms. So he converted to his own kind of Christianity. Within just a few years, he led the first army of Christians into war against other Christians. Jesus watched the conflict, and knew something had gone horribly wrong. Both sides were killing one another in his name, the name of a god who taught them to put away their swords and love one another.

When he confronted Inanna about this, she'd told him that the church would never expand to include all the people in the world if it held on to ridiculous ideals like extreme pacifism and universal forgiveness of sins. "Look, Honey," she'd said, "I'm committed to this whole 'Bride of Christ' thing. I'm going to make this work. That means every knee shall bow and every tongue shall confess that you are Lord. Or whatever. They'll all be on their knees with their tongues wagging, and that's the point. So you've got to man-up, recognize that it will be a bumpy road and I'm going to have to scratch the backs of some people you find unsavory. So let me do this thing, or get out of my way."

So he'd gotten out of the way. He'd moved back into his father's house (which was where he'd always felt most comfortable anyway, going back to when he was just a boy in Jerusalem), and he'd holed up in the basement and tried to ignore Inanna's perversion of his dream. Occasionally friends had dropped by to try to convince him it wasn't that bad.

"There are a bunch of people called 'Abolitionists' down there, Christians, your people, who are trying to put an end to slavery, Jesus," Baldur had reported.

"There's a bishop in South Africa who was not only instrumental in ending Apartheid, but he's bringing people together by having them confess their crimes on national TV and ask for forgiveness. This guy is one of yours, Jesus, no matter what Inanna has done," Apollo had said.

Of course, not all the messages were so good.

"Yeah, Inanna has a bunch of her people sailing across the Atlantic, making slaves of the people in North and South America, raping the women and killing the men, and given them all these diseases that are killing millions more. And of course her people all say they're doing it in your name. I know she's your wife, but Jesus, I hate that bitch," Artemis had told him.

"Firzzzt she had zzzem hating whatever paganzzz zzzey came acrozzzzzzzz," Khepri had told him. "Zzzzen mozzt humanzzz aczzzepted zzze illusion zzzat zzzey were monotheizzztzzz, zzzo she had zzzem hating zzze Chrizzztian Blackzzz. Zzzey hate zzze gayzzz and Jewzzz pretty conzzzizzztently, but now it zzzeemzzz she wantzzz zzzem to hate zzze Muzzzlimzzz zzze mozzzt."

"They're very strange, Inanna's Christians," Hephaestus said. "I get the impression that they spend most of their time trying to raise money to build fancy buildings. Then they gather inside to tell themselves that the people inside the building are better than the people outside the building. If they would decide that the people outside were just as beloved as the people inside, they could not only expand their numbers to include everybody, but save themselves a shit-load in building costs. I don't get them, Jesus. I really don't."

Jesus didn't understand Inanna's people any more than Hephaestus did, but loved them in the way a human would love a younger sibling with severe Tourette's syndrome who keeps shouting profanities and muttering gibberish; Jesus had to keep reminding himself that it wasn't their fault they made no sense or acted so inappropriately.

So he loved Inanna because she was his wife, but he also knew that loving her was like loving the cause of your little brother's crippling disability.

That made it a little tough to want to float over and shoot the breeze when he recognized her on the edge of the city, apparently waiting for him. When he got close enough to see that she was crying, he didn't take pleasure in her suffering, but he did feel confused. Was she that upset that he'd foiled this one little plan of hers? The Inanna he knew would have a dozen schemes going at the same time. Why would she be crying now?

He floated down to her. "What's wrong?" he asked. He didn't sound sarcastic or bored, but he couldn't manage to sound too compassionate, either, considering what she'd been trying to do recently.

"It's Toliq. She betrayed me."

Jesus frowned. "You're surprised? You surround yourself with these kinds of gods all the time."

Inanna shook her head. "Not like this, Jesus. It's madness. She's going to destroy us all."

"What?"

"Look!" Inanna pointed into the void behind him. He hadn't noticed the tiny shape floating beneath him as they'd crossed paths. Now he saw her in the reflection of the City's glow, the light bouncing off her trendy glasses, her bright red nail polish, her toothy smile, and her shiny hair. She was making the same gesture Enlil, Horus, and Ekkeko had made to call up Tartarus, and he could tell that she was muttering some incantation, though she was too far out for sound.

"What is she doing?"

"She's calling out to the gods who came before. The primordial ones. The ones who existed when your father's universe was only half formed. They will come back for revenge, Jesus, to destroy Asgard and Yahweh and every part of His creation. This is the end of all things."

"But why?" Jesus asked.

Inanna fell to her knees on the gold street and buried her face in her hands. The sound of her voice was muffled and mixed with sobs. "I don't know," she repeated over and over.

Apparently satisfied with her work, Toliq floated back, coming to rest just feet from them and staring at Inanna's hunched form with a pinched frown that squirmed between incomprehension and distaste.

Inanna looked up at her newest lover. Her voice was ragged and dry, almost a hiss. "What have you done?"

"Hey, no rain, no rainbow. You can't refudiate that."

"But Toliq, they will destroy us all! This is madness!" Inanna shouted.

Toliq cocked her head to the side like a confused dog and batted the long lashes behind her trendy glasses in two surprised blinks. "No it's not," she said. "It's just stupid."

"But Toliq!" Inanna said. She couldn't even think of anything to add to her reply for a moment because she was so flabbergasted. She took a careful breath and tried to explain. "Toliq, this kind of stupidity can destroy us. That's why it's madness."

"No," Toliq shook her head. "I refuse to believe that."

Inanna pointed to the tear off in the distance. It looked like a cinder in a dying fire, just specks of orange and red flame, but it was growing. "Open your eyes! Can't you see?"

Toliq did not look, but she rolled her eyes. "Oh, I see all right. I would have expected this kind of condescension from someone like Jesus or Yahweh or Frigga. That bitch always thinks she knows better than everybody else. But I thought you were on my side."

"I am on your side. But Frigga does know better. It's not condescension when you know the right answer, and I'm not trying to be mean when I say it's madness, what you've done. And I'm not siding against you when I point to something that will destroy us all!"

Toliq followed the line of Inanna's rigid arm, looking at the growing mass of fiery specks dribbling out of the rip in space. "I deny it. You are so nanny-state lamestream, Inanna."

"How can you deny what you see with your own eyes?"

Toliq smiled at her. "Oh, Inanna," she said, as though comforting a frightened child. "It's easy. You don't have to believe what you see with your eyes when you disagree with the people who tell you what it means. And I just disagree."

"Aagh!" Inanna turned to Jesus. "Can you help me?"

Jesus could only offer her a pitying look. "Save you from her? No. I don't have that much power. I used to think the unforgivable sin was denying the need for forgiveness. But now I see that it's more basic. It's not even refusing to recognize sin. It's refusing to think." He shook his head. "This was your plan. It all hinged on thoughtlessness. All your scheming and plotting and thinking...but the goal was always the absence of thought. And now you can't figure out a way out of the dead end path you created. And I can't save you from that."

"So what will you do?" Inanna asked.

Jesus clenched his jaw, closed his eyes, and breathed in deeply through his nose. He opened his eyes slowly and looked hard at his wife. "I will stand between Toliq's madness and my father's city. And I will die."

Before she could take some parting shot about how it wouldn't be the first time, or about how much she hated his martyr complex, he turned on his heel and walked down to where the particular suburban street of gold came to an end. He stepped off into the void and walked out into emptiness as easily as he might cross your average Sea of Galilee.

And there he was, alone in the void beyond Asgard, the space at the edge of heaven where nothingness wraps around like a gentle blanket. And where that blanket was torn, Jesus saw the creatures from beyond, the cast down, the eldritch gods of worlds before men and Earths before immortals. He was horrified in that darkness in a way no one living or dead or immortal can imagine. Arms bent and broken and healed badly scratched through the space in nothing, their claws shaped like the talons of vultures or the gripping pinchers of crabs or the mandibles of spiders pulling paralyzed meat into wet and groping mouths. The malformed gods pushed through the seam, some small and moving like colonies of advancing mold, but the large ones striding out to meet him with legs that bent the wrong way, wobbled, clicked, cracked and moved on. Waves of biting cold and searing heat rolled out ahead of them, and Jesus felt his flesh gripped by it, freezing and cracking and flaking off only to reappear, then blister and melt and slide off his bones into ashes. His bones themselves locked up like broken gears trapped by the sand of terror, and his mind was filled with the sound of the screaming he couldn't make his desperate, choking lungs produce. His eyes rolled around in his head, wildly taking in the army of incomplete deities clawing, dragging, and slouching their way toward the man from Bethlehem.

The ultimate pacifist didn't decide to fight. He didn't choose to kill. The rage came upon him from somewhere else just as it had that day he'd knocked over all those money changers' tables in the Temple. It was in his blood, an inheritance from a father who commanded men to kill children, a father who slayed all the firstborn in Egypt, a father who rained fire down on cities. Jesus' wild eyes discovered the shape in his hand before his fingers could communicate it to his brain, and he registered a tiny moment of unsurprise. Of course it would be that shape that is always a symbol of glorious battle, held in the air to direct the charging infantry, brought home and placed on the mantle to speak of nobility and courage, purchased at flea markets by young men who long for a midnight intruder to make them heroes, but in the heat of a real battle little more than an evolved stick to swing wildly at a charging rabid dog, a cross of steel.

Jesus swung the sword back and forth with no art or skill, just panicked warding, cutting a perimeter of space into which nothing could enter without consequence. And in that space he found just enough comfort to unlock his lungs and scream out his terror at the shapes that approached. He drove forward into the void, propelled by his own screaming, and then the blood and the cutting of meat gave shape to his bubble of fear. And in that space he cut and cut and stepped forward until his steps felt considered and then important. And the advancing army of nightmare shapes slowed in its approach, then stopped and watched as those closest to screaming Jesus lost their limbs and heads and fell and fell and fell on the bloody plains of the void, where they dripped down forever.

Once Jesus' loss became less certain, he gained allies. When Baldur and Apollo arrived, leading the tiny platoon of Thor, Artemis, Hephaestus, Sobek, and Khepri, they hesitated. But when Jesus' friends saw the armies of the eldritch gods slow and stop on the fields, and saw their friend isolated and mad with seeming-fury, they discovered their own seeming-courage in the shape of envy and insecurity. And so they took up their weapons and charged down around him, swinging hammers and axes, shooting their arrows of truth and justice and wisdom because they were too afraid not to. Now the eldritch gods felt a moment of hesitation and that was enough. The great terrors of the darkness are clownish enemies if they are also afraid. Their slinking motions became comical and pathetic, their dripping saliva just the drooling of idiots. And so the monstrosities turned and ran, those closest to Asgard running backward and clawing at the approaching gods as they went. And these were cut down, smashed, shot through with shafts of virtue desperate to find a place in the world. And the carnage was not glorious or epic or anything but the cutting of meat and the spilling of blood dripping down into the void forever and ever amen.

When the battle was over, Jesus, coated in the gore of a thousand half-formed gods, led his troop of immortals back to his father's city. He looked at the other gods and noticed their wounds. Thor only had a few scratches on his massive shoulders, and those were healing quickly. Sobek held one of his arms limp in the other, his elbow smashed, and blood ran from the place where one of his pronounced brows rose above his crocodile head. Something had nearly sheared off one of his raised eyes, but that, too, would heal. Artemis alone seemed completely unhurt. The others bore various stabs wounds from claws of different sizes. Hephaestus was fine while he floated, but Jesus thought he might limp on both his wounded legs, and wondered if that would even out somehow. There, on the edge of the island that was the City, they landed next to Toliq and Inanna. Jesus only recognized his own injury when his weight pressed down on the solid ground. He'd been stabbed in his side, just below his ribs. "Shit," he muttered. "Not again." He knew he'd be fine, but it hurt almost as much as the last time.

Baldur looked at the Aztec goddess of pestilence and mystery, the American goddess of anti-intellectual fundamentalism. "Should I cast her down to Tartarus?"

This woke Jesus from his contemplation of his wound. "Huh? No, you know I can't do that."

Artemis stared at him in disbelief, but Apollo shook his head. "Jesus is right. There would be no point. Nothingness cannot be undone, and ignorance is just the absence of knowledge. As long as there are gods, as long as there is power, there will be a will to ignorance. If we cast her down, it will just become the dominion of some other god." He sneered at her. "Better the devil we know."

"So she walks away from this with no consequences?" Artemis asked.

"Well, the best we can hope is that stupidity becomes less appealing," her brother said. "Thor, will you do the honors?"

"Huh?" Toliq said, taking a half step backward.

Jesus bowed his head. "Toliq, I want you to know, I take no pleasure in your pain."

"But I do!" Thor lunged forward and swung Mjöllnir. The wide head of the hammer smashed into Toliq's mouth, crushing everything from her chin to the bridge of her nose and sending the flesh and splintered bone up into her cavernous skull. The impact snapped her neck before it lifted her off her feet and tossed her whole body, flapping behind her head like a kite's tail, into the void over the edge of Asgard. She would come back eventually, of course, but she'd never be quite as pretty.

Toliq's trendy glasses fell on the gold street next to one of her shoes, just a few feet from Inanna, still on her knees, weeping.

The gods circled around Inanna. Jesus stood above her, looking down, his face as hard as stone. The other gods looked at one another and smiled.

"Muhammad was right," Jesus said.

He closed his eyes and took a deep breath.

"I divorce you. I divorce you. I divorce you."

25

Luke Devereaux sat at his gate at the Portland International Airport. People in Portland are ridiculously nice to one another, and Luke always found it necessary to immerse himself in a book to avoid any eye contact, because the people would inevitably nod or smile and he'd feel obligated to return their acknowledgment of his existence. He wasn't an unpleasant person, normally, but, in his present mood, he wasn't sure he wanted his existence acknowledged by anyone, himself included. Though he knew he was making the right choice in returning to New York, both personally and professionally, he couldn't help but feel he was going backward, running home to more comfortable environs with his tail between his legs.

Unfortunately, he'd chosen the wrong book to read. He'd never read any Christopher Moore before, but someone had given him a copy of *Fool* as a gift and hadn't warned him that it's the absolute wrong thing to read in a crowded place. It's just too funny, and the reader won't be able to keep from blurting half-stifled giggles. Worse, the laughter will be guilty, because the book in unabashedly bawdy. Consequently, Luke found himself looking around occasionally, trying to make sure no one was paying too close attention to him, just in case he laughed and earned a Portland smile or nod.

He didn't notice the man at the ticket counter, but something about the man's slouching pace caught Luke's attention over the top of the book. He lowered the novel and tried to catch a surreptitious glimpse of the man, then flushed when he was caught. The man did nod to him, but there was nothing happy in the man's expression. Then the man took the seat at the other end of the bank of three where Luke sat. He sat so heavily Luke felt the fiberglass bench jump a bit.

When the man sat down, Ixtab, who sat between them, had to grab her headdress which bobbled when she bounced. She took it off carefully and looked at this new man. Though she generally limited herself to writers, since their suicides were her purview, she couldn't help noticing this new man who looked like he wouldn't take much of a push.

As much as Luke wanted to avoid conversation, something about the man piqued that curiosity lobe that throbs in the center of a writer's brain and beeps, "Story. Story. Story." Besides, considering the man's expression, laughing at a novel in his presence would be adding insult to whatever injury he'd recently suffered.

"They giving you a hard time getting a seat?" Luke asked.

"No, no," the man said. He shook his head, then smiled slightly. "I haven't had any trouble flying all over the whole country."

"Business traveler?"

"Yes."

"What line of work you in?" Luke caught himself. "If you don't mind my asking."

"Pharmaceuticals. You?"

"Just placebos. I'm a novelist. Would-be, anyway." He put out his hand and leaned across the empty chair. "Luke Devereaux."

The man shook it. "Ghair Aadi."

"Your accent is interesting, Ghair. Where you from?"

Ghair Aadi looked at Luke carefully. "If I tell you, it may make you nervous to fly. I was born in Iran, lived in Saudi Arabia for a while, then moved to France."

Luke smiled. "Doesn't make me nervous. I know not all Middle Easterners are terrorists. But your English is very good. You never lived in the U.S.?"

"It's a popular second language to study in Iran, and I continued at university."

"Well, you speak it very well."

"Thank you. Your accent is interesting, too."

"I'm like you. Born in New Orleans. College in Iowa. Then lived in New York. I've only lived here in Oregon a little while, but I'm going back to New York. New teaching job."

"Congratulations."

"Well, we'll see."

Ixtab liked the sound of that. She looked over at Ghair Aadi to catch his reaction, and for the first time she noticed Meme standing behind him. She turned in her seat and gave a little wave. The god of absurd, post-modern religious atheism couldn't smile since he had no facial features, but he waved back.

Luke desperately wanted to ask Ghair Aadi why he looked so depressed, but he thought he'd already been too invasive with his questioning and couldn't figure out a direct way to bring up the subject. He decided to try another tack. He turned toward the stranger and threw an arm through Ixtab and over the back of the seat between them. "I don't know. I feel like I shouldn't be going back. Like I'm giving up and going home. Know what I mean?"

Ghair Aadi nodded slowly. "Yes. I do." He didn't elaborate, but in the silence he thought about his own predicament. He knew exactly how sick he should have been by then. Back when he'd made his plan, he suspected that by the time he reached LAX, he might have difficulty getting on to his next flight. He'd settled for the Portland layover to his flight to Hong Kong, though he'd wished they'd flown him through Seattle. Sea-Tac was a bigger airport with more traffic. He'd consoled himself that the authorities in Portland might be a bit less suspicious, and would wave him on to his flight even if he looked sweaty and had a runny nose. Once he was on the plane he could mask any vomiting as air sickness, but if he lost his lunch in a security line his trip would be over.

But by Atlanta he'd been suspicious, and in Chicago he'd known something was wrong. In LAX he'd given up and changed his itinerary. He'd decided to go back to New York, though he wasn't sure if he would continue on to Paris or take a few days there to re-assess his options. If he could get a hack license, it would be more fun to be a cabbie in New York than Paris. He knew people who might be able to help him get the status of his visa changed. Why not? Everything was fucked anyway.

"My plans have changed rather dramatically over the last couple of days," he said.

"Business trip isn't going well?"

"I think I'll be looking for a new job very soon."

Luke shook his head. "That bad."

"Well, maybe not all bad," Ghair Aadi said. He hadn't been bothered by the voices since he'd climbed on the plane in Paris. In London-Heathrow he'd spent a leisurely lunch at a large food court, listening to all the people talking and trying to hear his two auditory hallucinations over the din. He knew he looked strange, often looking up at the high ceiling, sometimes cocking his head to one side to hear. At the time he hadn't cared. He'd figured all the people who might choose to stare would be getting sick and dying shortly. The joke was on them. Now he knew the joke was on him. He wasn't sure if he missed the hallucinations. Had he cured himself somehow?

By the time he was flying between Chicago and Los Angeles, he'd begun to wonder if the hallucinations had gone beyond their auditory manifestations. After all, schizophrenics generally only heard voices, but some lost touch with reality in other ways. Despite popular belief, most schizophrenics were not a danger to anyone, but he'd nearly caused a mass-extinction event, so why shouldn't his hallucinations go beyond the norm, even for schizophrenics? Maybe it had all been a hallucination, or at least maybe all the biological work, the viruses, the dead mice, the injections.

"I'm beginning to question my professional judgment." Ghair Aadi looked down at his hands in his lap.

"Yeah," Luke said. "I get that."

They sat in silence. Ixtab's knee bounced with excitement at all the sorrow, and it made the headdress in her lap quiver, its feathers flapping wildly. Meme stood still, possibly disinterested, possibly asleep.

"You know, maybe we've been looking at things wrong," Luke said.

"How so?"

"Well, I write these books, and I want them to be this big deal. I want them to be meaningful and important. And you sell pharmaceuticals. You help heal people. Important stuff, right?"

"Sure."

"But maybe it isn't. Maybe the world needs another novelist as much as it needs another guitar player. And maybe pharmaceutical reps are a dime a dozen. No offense."

"None taken," Ghair Aadi said.

"So maybe we need to see ourselves differently. Find our meaning some other way."

"What do you mean?"

"Well, maybe I go back to New York and really devote myself to being the best teacher I can be. And maybe you go back and—"

"Become a cab driver?"

"Okay, sure. Or go to work for some big company that sells widgets or something. Or you take up watercolor in Central Park. Or whatever. And maybe we find nice girls and have families and devote ourselves to our kids. You married?"

"No."

"Me neither. Never wanted to be. But what the hell? Whatever we're doing, it's not working."

Ixtab looked concerned. She did not like this line of reasoning one bit. She looked to Meme for support, but his lack of a face was as expressionless as ever. He did shrug, though.

"You know, maybe we should just change our definition of 'working,'" Ghair Aadi said.

"How so?"

"Well, I'm starting to think I've been pretty self-absorbed."

Now it was Luke's turn to look down at his lap. "Yeah. Me, too."

"I've been an atheist all my life," Ghair Aadi continued, "but maybe there is a God. Regardless, religious people do a lot of good in the world."

"Some do."

"Right. So maybe I need to go find a religion." He smiled. "Something unconventional. Like Sufi or Bahai."

"Or Mormon or Scientologist?"

Ghair Aadi shook his head. "I don't think I could go that far." He thought for a moment. "I know! I'll convert to Judaism. Imagine, an Arab Jew from Iran who studied the Quran in a Wahabi madrasah."

Ixtab looked to Meme. He was clearly paying attention now, leaning over the back of the set of chairs and staring at Ghair Aadi.

"Sure," Luke said, laughing. "We could do it together. It'd be like a joke. An Arab and a swamp rat from New Orleans walk into a synagogue…"

"Exactly!"

"Maybe we could bring peace to the Middle East."

"Why not?"

"No less successful than my novels."

"Or my attempts to sell pharmaceuticals," Ghair Aadi said. Now he was really laughing.

Ixtab turned to Meme. "Should we just crash their plane?" she asked.

Meme shook his head slowly, then turned to her. His voice sounded like something run through a computer voice scrambler. "Plane crashes just make people pray harder."

"So we just give up on them?" she asked.

Meme shrugged. Then he slid over a few dimensions and ascended into heaven.

Ixtab hopped up onto her knees and leaned close to Luke. She put her lips so close to his ear he couldn't help but feel aroused. "You could have been glorious," she whispered. Then she kissed him on the cheek and followed Meme.

After she'd disappeared, Yahweh showed up, though only briefly. He stood behind the row of chairs and placed a heavy hand on the shoulders of the two men. He squeezed and blessed His newest converts. Then He returned to His city to talk with His son. He felt more hopeful than He had in a long, long time.

"You know, Ghair," Luke said, "you're right. We could still do glorious things."

Ghair Aadi smiled. His broad, genuine smile radiated a warmth he hadn't ever felt before. "I think I need to start with good things, first. If I get to great things, well…."

"…it would be a mitzvah!" Luke finished.

On the plane, they got as drunk as the airline would allow, and they laughed all the way to New York.

26

Yahweh sat next to Jesus on the old, stinky, corduroy couch in his basement. The TV was on. Celtics vs. Lakers. But it was a regular season game and both teams were leading their divisions, so they were only playing for playoff positions and possible home court advantage in the finals. It looked like Garnett was the only one who really cared who won. Even Kobe looked uninterested, even though he was halfway to a triple double. He was putting on a clinic in his sleep. Of course, the Celtics' "Big Three" were so old the real question was which one would break a hip first. Even God wasn't sure.

He felt the worn fabric of the couch cushions. The front edges of each cushion, once dark green, had been rubbed down to a soft, pale shade with a reflective sheen. He'd regretted giving Jesus the couch. He'd come to see it as a symbol of His son's depression, and He'd hated it. He'd wished He'd bought his son a flashy car instead. But now He realized He'd never spent any time sitting on the couch with Jesus. Maybe Jesus' prolonged depression had less to do with Inanna than God wanted to admit.

He patted the cushion and watched particles of dust dance up into the light of the television, reflecting the Laker yellow and purple, the Celtic green, and the beautiful hardwood of Boston Garden's parquet court. Yahweh knew the origin of every plank in that floor, and could identify the ones that were the originals, shipped up to Boston from a forest in Tennessee in 1946. The original floor was made in that parquet design because there was a shortage of lumber after World War II, and the East Boston Lumber company had been forced to use pieces from demolished army barracks. Die hard Celts fans might have known the history of what happened on that court, the 17 championships, the stretch of eight in a row, Red, Cousy, Russell, Cowens, Havlicek, Bird. But Yahweh knew every story of the wood beneath their feet. He watched Ray Allen dribble once before launching a perfect three-pointer, and thought about the board beneath that bounce, the barracks it had framed, the soldier who lived there. Private Hayes, an 18-year-old from Oklahoma, had sat under a beam made from that very piece of wood and had written a letter to the mother of his unborn child, telling her how much he would love that baby. Then he'd been killed on the island of Saipan. There wasn't a human being alive who remembered Private Hayes, his words, his love for a child he'd never met. But Yahweh knew.

Did it matter that he knew? God wondered. It didn't matter to Hayes (dead), his girlfriend (dead), or the child for whom he'd had such big plans (a miscarriage early in the third trimester). In fact, it didn't really matter to the living, either. The 16 living descendants of the four Japanese soldiers Hayes had killed on Saipan didn't give a rat's ass if Yahweh remembered the man who'd killed their grandfathers.

Yahweh looked over at his son. Maybe it mattered after all. Maybe he'd learned a little bit from Hayes, or at least from fathers who came before him. And maybe that enabled him to raise a son who kept on loving the hairless apes, and pulling their fat out of the fire again and again, no matter how many times they tried to wipe each other out. Maybe children make their parents matter in a way that transcends history, and death, and even memory.

"Does it still bother you when people pray about sporting events?" Jesus asked without turning away from the game.

"Not anymore. It bugged me when it was Christians and lions. Praying for injustice chaps my hide."

"Injustice to the Christians?"

Yahweh nodded. "And the lions. Both mine, and neither wanted to be participating in those games. But now? Sometimes I'm tempted to be petulant and pissy, to side against the prayers just to teach the fools a lesson. Like, right now, there's a guy in Milwaukee—"

"Robert Sousley," Jesus said.

"That's him. He's praying to you too, huh? Yeah, he bet his daughter's whole college fund that the Celtics beat the spread. Part of me wants to make a couple more of Odom's free throws drop. Celts will still win, but they wouldn't beat the spread. Maybe that would teach the guy a lesson. But I'm not going to bother, even if it does mean a big payday for that douche bag."

"He's just going to blow it all during the finals," Jesus said. "The guy has a problem. I feel sorry for him."

"I know you do," Yahweh said, but when he looked over at his son, he smiled. "You know I'm proud of you, don't you?"

"Thanks, Dad," Jesus said.

"So, how did you do it?"

Jesus picked up the remote and muted the TV, then turned to his father. "I showed up when Ghair Aadi called for a cab. I touched him, healed the sickness, and touched the samples he was going to throw in the trash. Then I just took him to the airport and let him go."

Yahweh shook his head. "You saved the human race as a cab driver. A fucking cab driver? You know I don't fully understand your love for them."

"I save, Dad," Jesus said. He shrugged. "It's just what I do."

Yahweh nodded. "So, what are you going to do next?"

"Well, now that I find myself a divorcé, I'm a bit conflicted."

"How so?"

"I have two plans at the moment. On the one hand, I want to try to reassert my values of love, tolerance, and forgiveness on humanity. I know that this will put me in direct competition with my own Church, since it's still under Inanna's control, but I think it's worth it. This time, I don't think I'll make everyone love one another out of obedience to me. That turned out to be a mistake. It was just too tempting for the ones spreading the word to take some of that authority for themselves, and that gave Inanna a perfect opening. In fact, when it comes down to it, I guess it's really all my fault. I gave her the Church, and I made the Church a symbol of authority. And, as you well know, authority corrupts. Present company excepted, of course."

God snorted, then rolled his eyes. "Yes, well, I've had my bad days, too. The occasional command to commit genocide, the odd city obliterated due to some indigestion."

"Exactly. And of course, the humans are weaker, and more prone to such things, when given even a smidgen of authority. So this time, I'll focus on them. Instead of Jesus Christ taking the side of the Christians, I think I'll take the side of the humans and be a Humanist."

God shrugged. "That sounds good to me. But you said you had two plans."

"Yeah." Jesus looked down at his feet, then kicked at something invisible and smiled. "It's a little awkward to tell your dad this…"

"What?"

"Well, I've been married but separated for a long time now, Dad."

"Yes?"

"So, you know, it's been kind of lonely…."

"And?"

"Well, I plan on making up for lost time. There's this stripper down at Bacchanalia. She's renamed herself Cherokie. With an "ie" at the end."

"I see."

"But I'm not planning on settling down. I've made that mistake. This time I'm going to play the field. Not a dozen wives, as my pal Muhammad suggested, but a few hundred friends-with-benefits, with a couple of other hundred one-night stands thrown in between. Dad, I plan on doing so much shagging that 'What would Jesus do?' becomes a pick-up line."

God slapped a heavy hand on Jesus' shoulder, then caught Jesus by the neck in the crook of his elbow and shook him. "I am so pleased to hear you say that." He released him a bit. "I say start with that plan, and take it slow with the Humanism stuff. It will win out in the end, I expect. People will realize that the ones who are more loving and tolerant and forgiving are just a lot better to be around, and the ones who claim to speak for us will increasingly look like crackpots who don't know what the hell they're talking about."

Jesus looked up at his father. "Do you really think so?"

God took a moment, then nodded slowly. "I do. I got tired of all that judgment and war and smiting. Even though injustice still gets my hackles up, I've generally found that sending armies off to destroy the wicked leads those very armies to become wicked, which defeats the purpose. It will take a few hundred years, maybe even a few thousand, but the humans will figure it out, too. Eventually they'll stop telling each other who is going to go to hell, then trying to send them there on their own. While they figure it out, I say you should enjoy yourself as much as you can. Eternity is an awfully long time, and I think boredom is the new unrighteousness."

"Well, Dad, if that's what you say, then that's enough for me," Jesus said. He turned and watched the game for a moment. Then he turned back.

"You know, Dad, I think you're the best dad a man can have."

God smiled. Then He thought about Joe and Dawkins.

"I think there might be some who are better." And that was it. He'd decided.

Jesus frowned. "Speaking of the whole man-having-God-for-a-dad thing, seeing as I'm fully God and fully man, do you think I'll live for all eternity, or just half?"

Yahweh shrugged. "To tell you the God's honest truth, I never fully understood that Myself."

27

The bell rang again. Yahweh, dressed in the body of Manny, walked into Andy's Coffee, made His way around the table by the door, and stepped up to the bar. He pulled off His heavy tweed coat and folded it more gently than usual, then set it on one of the barstools. Then He sat down on the stool next to Joe.

"How's it going?" He asked.

"Not too bad," Joe said.

"The usual?" Andy asked.

"Thanks, Andy," Yahweh said.

Joe noticed God's good mood. "What's going on with you?" he asked. He tried to sound casual.

"Had a close call, but things are looking up," Yahweh said. He decided not to mention that it had been a much closer call for Creation than for its Creator.

"Really?"

"Yeah, Jesus…." His voice trailed off when Andy returned from the kitchen. The shop owner set out two cups of coffee, then two napkins. He grabbed silverware and placed it on the napkins. Joe got the silver fork again this time. Then Andy set out the little bowl with the plastic cups of creamer inside, glanced quickly to make sure the porcelain holder was full of white, blue, and pink packets of sweetener, and nodded to his two customers before retreating to his kitchen.

Joe turned back to God. "So, Jesus?"

"He divorced his wife."

"That a good thing?"

Yahweh nodded slowly. "Yeah, it's a great thing, I think. He's out of the basement more, seems happier. He's talking to me again."

"He wasn't talking to you?" Joe asked.

"I wasn't talking to him. Not enough. It was my fault. I'm starting to think maybe all of it was my fault. But it seems like he's worked it out."

"Well, that's great," Joe said.

"Yeah, it is."

They sipped their coffees.

"So," Yahweh asked, "how about your situation with Christy?"

Joe placed the fingertips of his left hand to his lips. Why was he hesitant to explain this to God? he wondered. After all, He'd already know anyway. Still, something about discussing his marriage with anyone, even God, felt like a violation. He lowered his hand and ran his fingers along the handle of the silver fork.

"I think we've got it all worked out, too."

"Really?" God said. Frigga had not described her encounter with the Millers to her husband, and though God knew all about her radical decision to give up on her complete prescience, He hadn't pressed her about why she'd done it.

"Yeah. We really hashed things out. It was good."

"I'm glad to hear that," God said.

"Wow, what is up with you?" Joe asked. "I've never seen you in such a good mood. Jesus' divorce has really had an effect on you."

Yahweh sipped his coffee. "I guess it has," He said, smiling.

"Well then, you know I gotta ask. Have you made up your mind about that thing we keep talking about?"

"I have," God said.

"Really?"

"Yep."

"And?"

"Nope."

"What?"

"I said 'No.' A covenant is a covenant, and a curse is a curse. Fourth generation. That's what I said. Them's the breaks."

"But...."

"I enjoy our little meetings here, Joe. And, from what you say, Dawkins seems like a good kid. He'll grow up to be a good man, like you. I look forward to talking with him, too."

"But...." For a second, Joe was at a loss. He swiveled in his chair and stared hard at God. "But he won't be a good man. You'll wreck him. You'll ruin him, like you've ruined me. You'll make him bitter, like your goddamned coffee!"

251

Yahweh stared straight forward. "You're exaggerating. You're still a good man, and Dawkins will be fine. Besides, what do I care about one human's suffering?"

Joe could have explained that he was not the man he wanted to be, thanks to the curse. He could have explained that he wanted better for his son. He could have shouted that Dawkins was not just another human, not some statistic to be harmed at the whim of a dismissive prick of a deity. But these thoughts couldn't even form themselves in his mind, couldn't even take the shapes of words and explode from his mouth. Instead, every neuron in his brain shouted simple rage to the next. Muscles he never used contracted. Somehow, the fork shifted from his left hand to his right and turned over thanks to some brilliant primate muscle memory, but Joe was entirely unaware of this. When he lunged for Manny, he didn't know if he was going to strangle him or punch him or stab him. He didn't know the "man" was God. He knew nothing but a perfect wave of anger.

The four tines of the silver fork passed through God's shirt, then His flesh. They scraped against the inside of his clavicle, then sank deeply into God's body, just beneath His neck.

Then Joe pulled the fork back and stabbed again. And again.

The fork pierced God's chest, His shoulder, His neck, His cheek (passing just beneath the cheekbone, banging first against his rear upper molars, then hammering into his lower ones and forcing his mouth open before retreating to stab again), then the meat of His bicep.

Yahweh didn't raise His arms to defend Himself, but when the fork tore at His face, He turned His head. Then, when the next blow struck His arm, it spun Him on His barstool so that He faced Joe directly.

252

Joe placed his free left hand over the top of his right to maximize the force of each strike, and slammed the fork into God's chest three more times. The tines pierced the old man's sternum, penetrating his left lung twice, then his lower trachea.

The fork couldn't feel the tips of its tines tickling the top of God's beating heart. It was just a fork. But then, for the briefest moment, it was much more. A blinding white light appeared, filling the absence of the fork's consciousness, and suddenly the small metal utensil was the most enlightened object on the planet. It had one simple thought. "Om," it hummed.

Yahweh put out a hand and touched Joe's shoulder. Though the movement looked gentle, Joe was knocked to his knees. The fork was still embedded in Yahweh's trachea, just above his heart, and when He spoke there was a thick, bubbling sound. "That's enough," He said.

On his knees, tears stinging in his eyes, Joe gasped for breath. "Fuck you. I don't care. Kill me. I don't care."

"Oh, get up," Yahweh said.

Joe looked up.

God examined the handle of the fork sticking out of His chest, just beneath His lowered chin. He carefully wrapped His hand around the fork and pulled it straight out.

Oh well, thought the fork, then returned to unconsciousness.

Blood ran from God's cheek. Dark ovals formed on His shirt, His chest, His shoulder, His arm. A surprising gout of blood pumped out of the side of His neck, just once, and splashed down His shirt onto his lap. Joe's eyes followed the drop of blood that ran off the side of his leg and fell toward the carpet. When it made contact, the blood vanished like water on a hot grill, but without the hissing. Joe looked up at God.

"Take a seat, Joe," Yahweh said, and motioned to Joe's stool.

Joe rose slowly, then fell onto his barstool.

"I was just screwing with you," God said. "Your son is free. And you are too, for that matter. I'll leave you alone after today, if you want. The curse is lifted."

"But why...?"

"I needed that," God said. He coughed, and blood painted his bottom lip. He picked up his napkin, spilling His own silverware onto the counter, and coughed into it in a very human way. Then He stared at the blood on the napkin as He spoke. "A punishment maybe. No, a reminder. I haven't been taken to task like that since David, and he just chewed me out. I haven't been hit since Jacob. And that's too long. I've grown bitter. Like you say."

Joe tried to look at Yahweh, but it was too hard when His face was torn open like that, so Joe looked down at the counter in front of him. He glanced quickly toward the kitchen to make sure Andy wasn't coming out or calling the police, and that was when he noticed that the music had stopped. He could see Andy in the kitchen, turned so that Joe could make out his profile through the window. The shop owner was frozen, his expression calm. Joe looked around the room. Denise was also frozen, trapped in the act of filling one ketchup jar from another. Joe peered out through the restaurant's large front windows. Out on the street, two cars were also stopped, their drivers equally immobilized, hands on the wheel, eyes fixed on the road ahead. Above them, a bird hung in midair, its wings outstretched, perfectly still.

Then Joe risked another glance at Yahweh. Blood still ran from the wounds, but He didn't express any pain. Joe stared down into his coffee.

"You used me to hurt yourself. You're a dick."

"You can't hurt me, Joe. Not like that. But I couldn't just give you your freedom, your life. You needed to take your life back. Or throw it away to give Dawkins his."

"Don't pretend you did this for my sake. This was no gift," Joe said. "Look what you've done to me." His hands were shaking so badly he couldn't pick up his cup of coffee. Not that he would have taken a sip; the steam from the coffee was frozen above the cup, an unmoving wisp pointing at the ceiling.

"Maybe," Yahweh said.

The two of them sat in silence for a long moment in that place outside of time. Slowly, Joe's hands stopped shaking, and he rested them on the bar.

Finally, God spoke. "Joe, what will you tell Dawkins about me? Now that you are both free? Will you tell him I don't exist?"

Joe lifted his head and turned toward God very slowly. "I'll tell him you may exist, but I don't understand you."

"Hmm." Yahweh took a sip of His coffee. Blood and coffee leaked out of the hole in His cheek and ran down to His shirt.

"So, what now?" Joe asked.

"Your life belongs to you. Make it whatever you want."

"So, what, a happy ending?"

Yahweh shook His head and sipped His coffee. More of it ran out of His face.

"Don't trust those people who tell you things will all work out for the best," Yahweh said.

"But you made the universe good, right? So it has to end up—"

God interrupted by shaking His head.

"No, no. That's a common misconception. I made the universe, and then I called it good. I 'saw that it was good.' And you can look at it and see that it's good, too, if you feel like it. Or you can see that it's evil. I see it that way too, sometimes. Or you can see that it's orderly, or chaotic, or ridiculous. Whatever. I just made it."

Yahweh shrugged. Throughout the universe, galaxies shifted in their trajectories, veering slightly from the paths they burned across the void between the location of the Big Bang and their cold dissolution. The gravitational effect of the shrug was slight, but Joe felt a tightening in his stomach.

Yahweh leaned over the bar, resting on His forearms, and wrapped His hands around His cup of coffee. He lowered His head so that His shoulders were higher than His ears, and He looked over at Joe without turning, so that Joe could only see one of His eyes. It was wet, and grateful, and pleading.

"I don't know if it's good or bad. I don't know why things are the way they are. I just made it," Yahweh repeated. "I just made it."

Joe couldn't help it. The old man looked like a buffalo. Joe reached out and placed his hand on God's shoulder, comforting his Creator.

ABOUT THE AUTHOR

Benjamin Gorman teaches high school English in Independence, Oregon, where he lives with his beautiful, smart, and infinitely patient wife, Paige, and their essentially perfect nine-year-old son, Noah.

For more information, visit
www.TheSumOfOurGods.com

Made in the USA
San Bernardino, CA
27 May 2014